"I thought

Brady's grin he
what?" she aske

"To convince the courts to give me my son and you your house, our marriage will have to be... authentic."

Maggie opened her mouth, but her voice refused to work.

"In a custody hearing," Brady explained gently, "you could be asked if we'd—"

"Consummated the marriage," she finished weakly.

Brady smiled kindly. "It's the only way to guarantee we both win."

What, Maggie wondered desperately, had she gotten herself into? She had viewed the marriage as a business merger, nothing more. But if they made love... What if she let herself *believe* in love just because Brady McQueen held her against him... touched her...excited her...made her feel like his woman?

"So which is it, Maggie?" Brady prompted softly. "Yes or no?"

Dear Reader,

In the spirit of blossoming love, Special Edition delivers a glorious April lineup that will leave you breathless!

This month's THAT'S MY BABY! title launches Diana Whitney's adorable new series duet, STORK EXPRESS. Surprise deliveries bring bachelors instant fatherhood...and sudden romance! The first installment, *Baby on His Doorstep,* is a heartwarming story about a take-charge CEO who suddenly finds himself at a loss when fatherhood—and love—come knocking on his door. Watch for the second exciting story in this series next month.

Two of our veteran authors deliver enthralling stories this month. First, *Wild Mustang Woman* by Lindsay McKenna—book one of her rollicking COWBOYS OF THE SOUTHWEST series—is an emotional romance about a hard-luck heroine desperately trying to save her family ranch and reclaim her lost love. And *Lucky in Love* by Tracy Sinclair is a whimsical tale about a sparring duo who find their perfect match—in each other!

Who can resist a wedding...even if it's in-name-only? *The Marriage Bargain* by Jennifer Mikels is a marriage-of-convenience saga about a journalist who unexpectedly falls for his "temporary" bride. And *With This Wedding Ring* by Trisha Alexander will captivate your heart with a tale about a noble hero who marries the girl of his dreams to protect her unborn child.

Finally, *Stay...* by talented debut author Allison Leigh is a poignant, stirring reunion romance about an endearingly innocent heroine who passionately vows to break down the walls around her brooding mystery man's heart.

I hope you enjoy this book, and each and every story to come!

Sincerely,

Tara Gavin
Senior Editor and Editorial Coordinator

Please address questions and book requests to:
Silhouette Reader Service
U.S.: 3010 Walden Ave., P.O. Box 1325, Buffalo, NY 14269
Canadian: P.O. Box 609, Fort Erie, Ont. L2A 5X3

JENNIFER MIKELS

THE MARRIAGE BARGAIN

Silhouette®

SPECIAL EDITION®

Published by Silhouette Books

America's Publisher of Contemporary Romance

If you purchased this book without a cover you should be aware
that this book is stolen property. It was reported as "unsold and
destroyed" to the publisher, and neither the author nor the
publisher has received any payment for this "stripped book."

To my son
Thank you, Jeff.

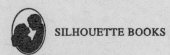

SILHOUETTE BOOKS

ISBN 0-373-24168-2

THE MARRIAGE BARGAIN

Copyright © 1998 by Suzanne Kuhlin

All rights reserved. Except for use in any review, the reproduction
or utilization of this work in whole or in part in any form by any
electronic, mechanical or other means, now known or hereafter
invented, including xerography, photocopying and recording, or in
any information storage or retrieval system, is forbidden without
the written permission of the editorial office, Silhouette Books,
300 East 42nd Street, New York, NY 10017 U.S.A.

All characters in this book have no existence outside the imagination of
the author and have no relation whatsoever to anyone bearing the same
name or names. They are not even distantly inspired by any individual
known or unknown to the author, and all incidents are pure invention.

This edition published by arrangement with Harlequin Books S.A.

® and TM are trademarks of Harlequin Books S.A., used under license.
Trademarks indicated with ® are registered in the United States Patent
and Trademark Office, the Canadian Trade Marks Office and in other
countries.

Printed in U.S.A.

JENNIFER MIKELS

is from Chicago, Illinois, but resides now in Phoenix, Arizona, with her husband, two sons and a shepherd-collie. She enjoys reading, sports, antiques, yard sales and long walks. Though she's done technical writing in public relations, she loves writing romance fiction and happy endings.

The honor of your presence
is requested
at the marriage of

Margaret Buchanan

to

Brady McQueen

on Saturday, October third
at four in the afternoon

Desert Chapel

Chapter One

"I'm here under duress," Maggie Buchanan reminded her brother as she sat beside him at a table in a posh Phoenix hotel ballroom. Outside, a cool September wind hinted of the rain and colder temperatures that announced the desert's approaching winter season.

Shifting on a chair, Bennett gave her a charming smile, one that usually weakened female knees. "You're here because I reminded you that this charity is near and dear to you."

"True, but I have no intentions of playing the game."

"You might have fun."

"Bidding for a date with a man?" Maggie asked with incredulity.

"It's for charity," he said over the wild clapping

and female screaming as the latest male, one of the city's hunkiest policemen, strolled onto the runway near the announcer's podium.

With disgust, Maggie viewed the gathering of mostly women, who, in her opinion, were making fools of themselves despite their well-dressed appearance. "Never," she said close to Bennett's ear. "Never will I do that!"

He chuckled and straightened the tie of his tuxedo as he regarded one woman seated at a nearby table. Sipping champagne from a fluted glass, she appeared more interested in him than what was happening at the auction. "Never say never, Maggie. Who is that?" he asked about the blonde.

"Elizabeth Hudson. She's the daughter of Judge Hudson."

"Maggie, do yourself a favor," he said, with eyes riveted on the woman. "Bid on the next guy." He spoke while never looking away from the judge's daughter.

Maggie delivered a frown at him. "What did you say?"

As if it took extreme effort, he dragged his gaze back to her. "You have a problem."

She needed no reminder of the dilemma she'd discussed with him during the taxi ride to the charity auction. "You aren't—you aren't suggesting that I...?" She caught herself talking louder and softened her voice. "Bennett, I am *not* going husband hunting."

"If you dated more, you might not be in this fix."

"I'm too busy." With a Ph.D. in Medieval History, she taught classes year-round at the university, she volunteered for several charities, and she belonged to the National Historical Preservation Society. She had no time for dating. "Most of the men I know are engaged, married, been there more than once or never plan to, so finding an eligible male is close to impossible, especially one who would want a short-term marriage," she said in her defense.

"Wrong. I know one," Bennett cajoled, giving her his full attention now. "I happen to know that Brady—"

"Brady? Brady McQueen?" It wasn't that she was easily impressed by a man's looks or his hard body, but Brady McQueen with his sexy smile and intense blue eyes had garnered the tag of any woman's dream by every eligible female in Bennett's and her social crowd—and probably every woman he ever met. But Brady McQueen preferred delicate-looking blondes like Kirsten Scott, his late wife, or the slinky one ogling Bennett.

"He's receptive," Bennett said, cutting into her thoughts.

"Receptive to what?"

"And you might even enjoy being romanced."

She couldn't believe he'd come up with some lamebrain solution to her problem. Eight years older, her brother usually acted more sensible. As a lawyer, he'd always conveyed an abundance of common sense and logic. He suddenly seemed lacking in both. "I don't want romance."

"Which is why you're in this fix," he told her.

Feeling as if her brother's intelligence had dropped several notches, she measured her words. "Tell me. Why would he want to be my husband?"

"A date, Maggie. That's all I'm suggesting." In an exasperated manner, he raked a hand through hair as dark as Maggie's.

"Why?"

"Because it might lead to more."

"Get real, Bennett," she said louder than necessary, turning heads toward them.

He chuckled. "I love it when you forget public propriety."

Between gritted teeth, she whispered, "This is ridiculous."

"It's not. I told you earlier that you have no choices. You need to get married." His gaze drifted to the blonde again.

Patiently, Maggie waited while he delivered another toe-curling smile. No wonder Bennett and Brady were friends. They came from the same man-about-town mold. While on more than one occasion she'd enjoyed watching her brother's flirtatious moves, she never intended to fall prey to such a heartbreaker.

"A husband is what you need."

Uneasy with the topic, Maggie looked up in response to the screams of women. Dressed in a tuxedo, his grin in place, Brady waited for the applause to end.

"Maggie." Bennett snapped his fingers in front of her.

Blinking, she scowled over her own mesmerized response to Brady.

Bennett had the good sense not to make an issue of her reaction. "The bidding is up to seven hundred," he said instead.

Amazing, she mused. Why would intelligent women make such fools of themselves?

"There aren't too many places to meet men," he said in a prodding manner. "Single bars, personal ads." At her scowl, he laughed. "I'm not serious."

She should have known better. He, of all people, knew she wouldn't resort to such action. She never took unnecessary chances. She drove with car doors locked. She never walked anywhere after dark, and she carried defense spray with her always. Most important, she never dated impulsive, pleasure-seeking men hell-bent on thrills.

"Finding a husband is a serious business."

"Exactly. One that I don't want," she muttered.

"This isn't about what you want," he said softly. "This isn't meant to be forever. It's a solution to your problem." He placed fingers under her chin and angled her face toward the runway and the man on it. "Bid," he insisted.

"Not without knowing what you're talking—"

"We don't have time for explanations. Bid now. Or you'll ruin the plan."

Maggie swung a questioning look at him. "What plan? Whom do you have a plan with?"

His head jerked in Brady's direction.

"You discussed me?" Had he really told Brady about poor Maggie with no marriage prospects?

"Bid," he ordered.

"Not without knowing what you said to him."

"He needs you, Maggie."

Not fair, she wanted to yell. He knew her weak spots. If someone needed help, call Maggie. She couldn't say no. "Ladies," the emcee urged, "here's your chance for a date with a sexy, intelligent man. He's offering a dream date. Is it a romantic dinner on a yacht at sunset, a horseback ride at sunrise, an evening at the symphony or a day of skydiving or wind surfing? The choice is yours with this bachelor. He can do it *all*''

"One thousand," Maggie said loudly. Heads swiveled in her direction. Fighting a blush, she ignored a striking brunette's glare.

Immediately the woman upped the bid another two hundred.

"This is crazy," Maggie whispered to her brother.

"It's for charity. Make it fifteen."

"Fifteen hundred," Maggie said, amazed her voice sounded stronger this time.

The brunette's glare intensified, but she remained silent.

Maggie heard the emcee carrying on about a date worth the money. Then, smiling, Brady was strolling toward her, looking alert, ready for action.

What kind of action, Maggie wasn't sure. Her stomach fluttering, she wanted to slink to the door. That wouldn't do. So what if he was strong and self-assured? So what if her tongue felt tied? With every ounce of willpower she possessed, she met his stare squarely.

"Hi, Maggie," he said in that smooth and throaty-sounding, butter-would-melt-in-the-mouth voice.

She was in trouble, she knew instantly. No one had ever made her name sound quite so romantic, said it so sensuously soft. No one had ever spoken her name and sent a shiver down her spine. She wished she could think of something to say. She was intelligent, and with most people, a fairly good conversationalist. But he wasn't most people.

He was Brady McQueen.

Sandy-colored hair, cut casual and sun-bleached around his face, accentuated the firm planes of his face, strongly chiseled and suntanned. Faint lines at the corners of his eyes added character to his rugged good looks. He was outgoing, a local sportswriter for the *Herald*. From what Bennett had said about him when they'd first become friends, Brady had a background and life-style that differed greatly from Maggie's reserved, affluent one.

Maggie caught her brother's questioning stare at her silence. "What exactly is going on?" she asked.

"Why don't we leave?" Brady suggested. Airing his problems with so many alert ears nearby made no sense.

"Give me one minute," Bennett said, standing.

Maggie snagged his arm. "Bennett..."

"I'll be right back," he promised.

She released her hold on the sleeve of his tuxedo.

Brady could have eased her obvious embarrassment, backed away and let Bennett arrange for a meeting tomorrow. But something about her reserve made him plant his feet firmly. "We could step outside? Get away from all of this." She looked nervous but controlled. In fact, he thought, that word described the proper-looking Ms. Margaret Buchanan perfectly.

Maggie noticed her brother scribbling the sexy blonde's phone number on a napkin. Aware of the attention she and Brady had garnered, she'd have flown to the door if possible. Head high, back straight, she strolled toward the exit. Around them, heads turned and voices buzzed with whispered questions. Inwardly she groaned, certain she would be the main topic for gossipers over their breakfast tomorrow.

"You need a husband," Brady said quietly as they left the ballroom and stepped into the quiet hotel lobby.

She'd kill her brother—tomorrow. Right now, she wished for the floor to open and let her disappear.

"Don't be angry at Bennett," Brady soothed. "I have a similar problem. I need a wife."

She saw no problem. Men like him could get one easily, if they wanted one. She stopped the thought. He'd said he needed a wife. Brady hadn't used the word *wanted*. She looked up to see Bennett ambling toward them. "Explain now," she insisted when he drew near.

"As your brother, and Brady's friend and lawyer, I'm aware you both have legal problems. Brady needs someone like you, Maggie. Not some bimbo," he added with a glance at Brady.

Instead of helping her solve her problem, her brother had donned the role of matchmaker. "You've become certifiable, Bennett," she returned, with the same I'll-not-be-pushed-around tone she'd leveled at him while they were growing up.

"Maggie, you're not thinking. To get what you want, you need Brady."

She shook her dark head. "When you told me to come here, that you had a solution, I assumed you'd discovered some legal loophole in the trust."

"No such luck. No loophole. To get what you want, you have to get married."

"I don't want to get married, ever," she reminded him. Peripherally, she felt Brady's gaze on her, almost decipheringly, as if he were waiting for an explanation. "You know how I feel," she said to her brother. "I came here hoping for help, and this is your perfect solution?"

Brady couldn't take his eyes off her. When she got going, she was something. Passion brought a glow to her fair, oval-shaped face, and darkened those eyes that were as blue as a stormy sky. Framed by long, dark lashes, they looked annoyed. He knew from others that she was viewed as a quiet, reserved, even prim woman. But a glimpse of her passionate nature held a promise of more waiting, only needing to be fanned.

"It's a good idea," Bennett said defensively.

It's insane." Maggie turned a look on Brady. Unwittingly, she felt tiny pinpricks of sensation flutter down her spine. "You aren't seriously considering this, are you?"

"I think it would work." He liked people, all ages, all kinds. He knew his neighbors, called his doctor and the mechanic who puttered under his car by their first names, and he talked often to the kid who threw his newspaper every morning with amazing accuracy into a prickly pear cactus near his front door.

Others viewed Margaret Buchanan as affluent, cultured, even a little uptight. This woman with her shiny, raven-colored hair pulled back neatly and gathered in a clip was everything he needed in his life. She was perfect. She was *respectable*.

Bennett raised his hands as if warding off evil and backed up toward the ballroom door. "Think about it, Maggie."

Pure panic rippled through her as Bennett whipped around and started for the double doors that led into the ballroom. "Where are you going?"

"You don't need me here now." His hand on the doorknob, he winked back at her. "Talk it over." He disappeared quickly in his eagerness for more conversation with the blonde.

Maggie vowed to strangle him tomorrow. "This is crazy." How could her brother even introduce her to a man who'd led a life as wild and undisciplined as hers had been cautious and reserved? In the past, she'd chosen the predictable, the unadventurous. She didn't need a brash, daring man who, even if not now but earlier in his life, had walked on the wild side of life.

"Bennett didn't tell me why you need a husband. Let's have coffee in there," Brady suggested, and gestured toward the hotel's coffee shop.

She had better things to do than explain this to him.

Though mindful of manners that had been drilled into her, she squared her shoulders and offered a shake of her head as a response. She was not baring her soul to him of all people.

"Come on, Maggie." He bent closer, so close the heat of his breath caressed her face. "I'll be honest," he said so softly she nearly strained to hear him. "I'm desperate."

Maggie couldn't believe he'd ever said that to anyone.

Didn't people like him lead charmed lives, where everything was always perfect?

"You knew about Kirsten, didn't you?" Brady asked.

Underhanded or not, he appealed to her compassion. Right now, he would do anything, absolutely anything to get her help.

Maggie nodded at his reminder that he'd endured more than a little disappointment in life. He'd tragically lost his wife. "I don't understand what this has to do with her."

Before he replied, Brady studied Maggie carefully. She wore a black dress, high at the neck with long sleeves, and a single strand of pearls. She looked so proper. He remembered having the same thought in the ballroom that had been filled with women wearing glittering finery. "Level with me first. Tell me why Bennett felt you'd be willing to discuss marriage with me."

With his face so near, she observed a small scar on his cheekbone. "I haven't the vaguest idea."

Brady took her hand in his.

Maggie wanted to tug it back, but he shifted so she couldn't pass by without brushing against him.

"Did you get yourself in some kind of mess?"

"I assure you, it's nothing I've done," she said, sounding offended.

Unlike him, Brady reflected. He was in a mess of his own making. No, he figured sensible Maggie had never done anything impulsive in her life.

"My grandfather—" Maggie paused. She had a difficult time believing that the sweet old man she'd loved more than anyone else in the world had done this to her. "Before he died several months ago, he set up a trust for me." She moved forward at the urging of Brady's hand beneath her elbow and strolled with him into the coffee shop.

So far Brady didn't see a problem. Most people viewed an inheritance as good news.

"There's a ludicrous clause in it," Maggie said when they were settled at a table.

Brady ordered coffee, watching her lips tighten with that peeved look again just from mentioning her problem. Maggie assumed without some background explanation he would view her dilemma as hardly worth mentioning. "For years, I lived with my grandfather. He had a wonderful old Victorian house."

Brady nodded a thanks as coffee was set before them. He made an assumption. A shy woman. The world of an elderly grandfather was safe and sedate. No stretching her wings like other women her age. "Is that your home now?"

"Of course not. I left when I was twenty-two and got my own apartment."

Never assume anything, he reminded himself.

Maggie sipped the steaming brew, then went on. "The house is in that trust until my thirtieth birthday."

"You're going to be thirty?" He grinned slowly, a corner of his mouth curling. "You look younger."

She understood his success with women. He hadn't taken his eyes off her. He knew how to make a woman feel as if she were the only one in the world. "I'll be thirty at the end of November. So I have barely two months," she said, more stiffly than she'd intended. But she felt as if she were clinging by her fingertips to keep her mind on the business at hand. "Actually, about eight weeks from now."

"To get married?"

Maggie avoided his stare. "Yes. The house is mine then if—"

"What if you're not married?" To him, a house was only a building. Apparently, for her own reasons, the house meant more to her. "What happens to the house then?"

"It goes to my cousin Cassandra Walerford and her husband Anderson."

"Walerford." Brady lounged back in the chair. "That's your cousin?"

"No, his wife is," Maggie repeated. "Née Cassandra Kentington, and she is certain she'll get the house. Because she and Anderson know I—" This was humiliating. "They know that I don't have a prospective husband hanging around."

His eyes narrowed as if he were trying to see beyond what was visible. "Why don't you, Maggie?"

"Pardon?"

"Why don't you?" He rested a forearm on the table and fingered a loose raven strand with his other hand.

Something unexpected and warm spread so rapidly through her that Maggie had no time to block it. "They're counting on my—" She wished he would stop doing that. Feather light, his knuckles brushed her cheek. "On my single status so they can sell to an interested buyer."

"The house is valuable?" He let his fingers trail down to her slender jaw. On every inhalation, he smelled a subtle scent, like flowers in bloom after a springtime rain.

Maggie barely focused on his question. "The property is."

She heaved a sigh of relief as he drew back. "I hadn't realized how much my grandfather let the house deteriorate. It needs some restoration. Once it is restored to its original beautiful state—"

"Which is what you want to do?"

For no reason except she needed to grip something, Maggie reached for the small black clutch purse in her lap. "Yes, it is."

"Go on."

Nerves danced again as he gave her his undivided attention. "Then the historical society will add it to its list for the Historical Homes Tour."

"So you don't want to live in it?"

"No, not really. I want it to be preserved, treasured. It's a grand house, and I had so many wonderful memories there."

"And if you don't get the house, then what happens to it?"

"I've no doubt whomever Cassandra sells the house to will bulldoze it and put up an office building, since it's near the city's prime commercial section."

And there wouldn't be anything tangible to spark her memories.

"Cassandra and Anderson want—"

"Wait a minute. Cassie and Andy." He grinned with private amusement. "I do remember them. Kirsten invited them to a fund-raiser party." Clearly he recalled the supercilious pair who'd sipped champagne between conversations dominated by the word

I. "There's something I don't understand." He leveled a more serious look at her. "Why does this bizarre clause about your being married by your thirtieth birthday even exist? If your grandfather loved you, why did he do this?"

She kept wondering, too, how he could have done this to her. "My grandfather had a romantic soul," she said, using the only explanation she could think of. "He was married forty-five years. He believed in love and marriage, and knew I didn't."

Who'd broken her heart, made her distrust all that others yearned for? For the moment, Brady kept the question to himself.

"Before he died, he must have thought I'd be terribly lonely."

"Because you're alone?"

"Yes, he would think that." Maggie followed his hand's movement as he lifted his coffee cup. Disturbingly, she realized she could still recall the heat of his touch. "I'm sure he believed that I would closet myself in the house, restoring it."

"Would you?"

"It doesn't matter."

She would, Brady guessed.

"Thus, the clause was an incentive for me to get married."

And he couldn't just leave her alone and let her get married when she was ready because he'd sensed she wouldn't ever be ready. Brady studied her face, the high cheekbones, the soft curve of her lips. "I'm having trouble understanding how you can be so sure marriage isn't for you."

"I knew when I was twelve that I didn't want it."

Brady wondered if she'd made the same declaration at that age, raising that pointed chin of hers to exactly the same stubborn angle. "Don't like kids?"

"I like children. They have nothing to do with my decision."

It became clearer to Brady why Bennett had pushed them together. "Let me get this straight. You don't plan to fall in love. That's what you're really saying, isn't it?"

"Something like that." Maggie shook her head to stop the waitress from refilling her coffee cup. "So you know now why I need to get married, but why do you?"

"Guess it is my turn." Brady didn't want to explain too much, not yet, not until he knew she was committed to helping him. "My wife's mother is Olivia Elliot Scott."

Maggie had met the woman at several social functions.

Olivia Elliot Scott was a stern, sour-faced, influential woman with a sharp tongue. Maggie couldn't recall ever seeing the woman smile.

"She wasn't bashful about her dislike of me, or her opposition to Kirsten marrying me."

Maggie wasn't following. What did his late wife's mother have to do with this absurd plan?

"Olivia wants Conor."

"Conor?" Maggie focused on him.

"That's my son."

A child was involved in this?

"You look surprised."

She would never have imagined him as a father. "How old is your son?"

"Twenty-three months."

A baby. "So Mrs. Scott has custody now?"

"Temporary."

Maggie was curious how she got that, but innate politeness kept her from questioning him.

"She wants permanent custody."

"Oh, I see."

How calmly she'd said that. Brady doubted she understood anything, especially how desperate he was to get Conor back. This might prove more difficult than he'd anticipated. How could he explain his concern for Conor having to live under Olivia's autocratic and austere rule?

"I do see your problem. What you can offer your son pales in comparison to the wealth and obvious social status Olivia has."

And Brady knew she would stifle every imaginative bone in Conor's body, steal away his ability to laugh.

Maggie was torn. Would a little boy fare better with a father who possessed a bachelor-on-the-loose reputation?

"This brings us back to what I guess is Bennett's idea," Brady said with a mirthless laugh. "If you marry me, I get a wife whom the court will view as acceptable. I'll win custody of Conor." He said it calmly, but his stomach knotted whenever he considered the possibility of losing. "And you'll be able to fulfill the stipulation in that trust. You'll keep the house."

How simple he made it all sound. "You're suggesting a business deal," she said, rising. "A marriage bargain."

He stood close. "I'm talking about the welfare of my child. Which is why I'm desperate. My son belongs with me," he said quietly, though he wanted to shout the words at her. "Think about it." He reached back, flipped open his wallet and set money on the table. He'd presented his problem. No more needed to be said. "This idea would solve problems for both of us."

And create what new ones? Maggie wondered while watching him saunter to the exit.

Chapter Two

Brady considered himself lazy. He liked to sleep late whenever possible, but forced himself from bed for a morning jog. He had the lean, muscled body of an athlete, though he spent more time watching sports than playing them now. At six foot two, he'd been a natural athlete, but too many jolts to his right kneecap during football games had killed a pro career in football, so he'd chosen journalism instead.

He worked at home more than at the newspaper. When he'd needed to attend games, get interviews or leave town, he hadn't needed to worry. He had a housekeeper. Responsible, trustworthy, even grandmotherly, Irene Bonner had worked for him since before his marriage to Kirsten. No, he would have no worry about Conor's welfare. That wasn't a problem. Getting his son back home was.

Right now, his sports column demanded his full attention.

Sporting events, airplane schedules and newspaper deadlines controlled his life. This morning he faced an important one. Besides his biweekly sports column, he'd been working on a series that included interviews with basketball players who'd been on the road of recovery after drugs. A human-interest piece, it was meant to promulgate one message to kids who viewed such men as role models—drugs shorten sports careers. Instead of faxing it in, he'd come to the newspaper that morning to collect his paycheck.

As he stepped from the elevator, munching on breakfast, a police beat reporter scurried by. "Big break in the Tobin case," he yelled while punching the elevator button with one hand and popping an antacid in his mouth with his other.

"Good luck." Brady strode with an easy gait toward the newsroom. He rarely endured such stomach-knotting moments, and wondered how some reporters lasted a career lifetime at the job.

Turning, he nearly plowed into a tall, leggy brunette who worked in research. He smelled her perfume, something strong and lingering, and oddly thought about the lighter, flowery scent that Maggie wore.

He'd given her two days to consider the business proposal. Two days was his limit for a lot of reasons. Mostly, he'd been wanting to see her again. Maybe she interested him because she didn't want any emotional involvement, didn't want marriage. That made her perfect for him.

"Morning, Brady."

He greeted Tina Kostowski with a smile. She had everything in the right places to make a man drop to his knees. Brady had dated her a few times, but backed off out of fairness to her. What he needed was an arranged marriage, a short-term one that could be dissolved without complications.

Inside the large newsroom with its rows of desks, bedlam reigned. Keyboards clicked, phones rang, voices buzzed. At the desk across from his, Charlie Bigelow exaggeratedly sniffed and muttered under his breath around the stub of the fat cigar in his mouth. "What in the blazes are you eating at nine in the morning?"

"A chili dog." Brady plopped on his desk chair and scanned an interoffice memo about cutting expenses.

"I used to do that when I was your age," Charlie grumbled almost wistfully. He ran a hand over his bald head. "That was when I had as much hair as you do. Fast living will be your downfall, McQueen."

Brady already knew just how much could be lost. His frown lingering, he scrunched a scribbled phone message from a football player's press agent. They'd talked yesterday. He aimed the balled paper at the wastebasket beside his desk and gingerly tossed it in. For a long moment, he stared at the next note. "Did you take this message?" he asked while trying to decipher Charlie's chicken scratch.

Charlie threw him an over-the-glasses glance. "Yeah." Seeming aware of his own lack of good penmanship, he added, "The last name is—"

"I know what it is." A tightness coiled inside Brady's stomach. He felt edgy, and until that moment, hadn't realized how much he'd hoped to hear from Maggie, how much he'd been counting on her being his savior.

"Nice voice."

"What time—" Brady never bothered to complete his question. Instead, he enjoyed Maggie's approach. Long-legged, she wore tailored, classic clothes. A taupe-colored blazer hid curves that the creamy white, cowl-necked sweater beneath it might have revealed. Trim-cut, taupe slacks showed no suggestive line of her feminine contours. She carried herself like a princess, and he wondered how many hours at a finishing school she'd practiced walking with a book on her head to accomplish perfect posture.

Without looking away from her, Brady finished the last of his chili dog and shoved everything off his desk and into a drawer. "Hi, Maggie."

Maggie had thought if she initiated the second meeting she would feel less jittery; she'd been wrong. No wonder women's heads turned and their fantasies began when he entered a room. She thought that he must be aware of the impact he had on women. An Atlanta Braves T-shirt accentuated his lean, muscled body and broad shoulders. With long, denim-clad legs stretched beneath his desk, he looked tough, like a man who would challenge his body and test his fate to discover if, like a cat, he had nine lives.

Brady rose and stepped around his desk. "You came to say yes?" he asked hopefully. He needed her. She had no idea how much.

"I came with questions," Maggie returned.

He supposed it was foolish to expect her to automatically say yes after their brief conversation the other night. "Such as?"

Maggie was alert to the curious look of the man seated at the nearby desk. "Can you leave?"

"In a minute." Brady stretched back and punched a key on his computer.

Disturbingly, Maggie found herself mesmerized at the sight of the denim following the curve of his tight backside.

"All set." When he pivoted toward her, he read uneasiness in her eyes. She didn't want to be here. Yet she'd come. Feeling encouraged, he asked, "Want to get some breakfast?"

Her gaze darted in the direction of the wastebasket and the chili-stained wrapper. "Didn't you just finish eating?"

"A snack."

"I'm not hungry." She was nervous. She was considering a step so out of character for her that her legs threatened to buckle beneath her.

He ignored her uncooperativeness. "I'm glad you came by. I was going to call you today." Behind him, he heard the squeak of Charlie's chair and knew he was unabashedly eavesdropping. "I owe you a date."

Maggie had totally forgotten about the auction date.

"Why don't we discuss it outside. There's a garden and some benches for employees there."

He slipped a hand beneath her elbow. It was a casual touch, but he stood close. While murmurs of his co-workers accompanied their walk through the newsroom to the exit, all she could think about was the heat of his body.

When he opened the door at the exit, she rushed

out ahead of him. A cool late-September breeze ruffled palm fronds. Though she concentrated on the plethora of petunias planted in several flower boxes, there was no ignoring what he did to her, which made this whole plan more unthinkable. "Why me?" she asked bluntly, needing to know.

Brady stopped her with him at one of the redwood picnic tables. "What do you mean, why you?"

"You could choose any woman you wanted." She sat across from him. "It's a known fact that there are several women who would jump at the chance to be your wife."

"But they'd expect something." Brady settled across from her. As necessary as this marriage was, it needed to be free of emotional involvement. "If I asked one of them, she would assume that I did so because I love her."

"Not if you explained that you wanted a business arrangement."

Brady chuckled, though he wasn't feeling so lighthearted at the moment. "If I asked one of the women I've been involved with, she wouldn't believe that."

"You couldn't love any of them?"

Love? A gut-wrenching emotion. "No, I couldn't." He didn't want to. Once was enough to feel himself ripped open because of love. "You would expect nothing from me, except a bogus marriage. And you're not like any of them. You're very—"

Maggie raised her head to meet his gaze squarely. She prided herself on being perceptive. "Proper?"

Brady didn't want to hurt her feelings, but above all else, he needed to be honest with her. "That's right. You're the most proper woman I know."

For the first time in her life, she wished someone would call her 'beautiful.' Or say she was exciting, stunning. Foolish thoughts, she knew. She didn't want romance or fair words. She didn't want men ogling her. She would never be a woman whose life revolved around men. But she couldn't help wishing *he'd* said one of those words to her, this man who could have almost any woman he wanted.

"Maggie, that was a compliment."

She managed a slip of a smile. Yes, she supposed it had been. But still— She mentally shrugged. She couldn't change what she was. Some people had used the word *pretty* to describe her. She'd even been called sweet. She did have high ideals that she rarely wavered from. But then, she'd had plenty to live down. She couldn't afford to be the kind of woman people talked about. They'd talked enough about her mother.

Brady worried about her silence. She needed to understand how appealing that particular character trait was to him. "My reputation needs whitewashing, Maggie."

She met his gaze, understanding now that her part in this scheme entailed repairing his reputation. From Bennett, she'd learned that Brady possessed a risky, adventurous nature. For years, he'd mountain climbed, skydived, lived on the edge.

"I've stupidly provided Olivia with enough ammunition to petition the court for permanent custody of Conor."

Because of womanizing? Maggie wondered. "Yes, I suppose you have." Was that how he'd lost custody of Conor?

As she sat there, so prim, with her hands folded in her lap, an urge swept over him to reach forward, grab her and plant one hard, mind-boggling kiss on her. Seeing that frown line between her brows again, he asked, "You have another question?"

"How did Olivia get temporary custody?"

Tension tightened his shoulders. He couldn't tell her everything. He couldn't bare his soul to a stranger, to anyone. He couldn't share what he'd carried with him for so long now that it seemed attached to him.

"Brady?"

She was asking for him to remember some painful moments.

He had little choice. He supposed that she needed to know what a fool he'd been. "I was out of it after Kirsten died. That's no excuse. It's simply the truth. I was numb." He averted his gaze from the blue eyes intent on searching his. "I couldn't take care of myself, much less my son. When Olivia took him, I didn't resist. I thought Conor would be better off with her." He was dodging the truth expertly. She would accept what he'd said, but he was leaving out what really mattered. "I used to act on my feelings a lot." And believed to hell with the consequences.

For someone who mulled endlessly over every action, she had difficulty understanding people like him.

Unwilling to bare his transgressions, Brady shifted uncomfortably. She kept staring at her hands resting on the top of the table. Narrow-fingered, delicate-looking hands. "What are you thinking about?" he asked, because she looked so lost in her thoughts.

"About what you'd said. What exactly have you

done that Mrs. Scott might use to persuade the court that you're an unfit parent?''

I wasn't there for my wife when she needed me most. ''She could make a lot of things seem worse than they are,'' he answered.

''Such as?''

Brady blew out a long breath. ''There was a mountain-climbing trip at Mount Everest. It wouldn't take much for the courts to learn I was there instead of with Kirsten when she had Conor.''

Maggie's back straightened. She wanted to think the best of him, but even to her he sounded selfish and insensitive.

Brady didn't like being on the defensive, having to explain everything to her, but she was the woman he wanted—no, *needed.* Without her, he might never get Conor back. ''The baby came early, or I'd have never left town.''

She hated the need to challenge him, but she couldn't accept his past with no explanations. She never understood how someone could be an attorney and defend a guilty person. If she was going to be his wife, be his support against Olivia, she needed to know everything and believe in him. ''How early?'' she asked, determined not to prejudge him without all the facts.

''A week.'' He noted her frown deepening the line between her brows and was tempted to place a finger to it, wishing that with a touch he could ease it away. ''Let me explain. A friend was on the expedition. When he was reported missing, I joined the search team.''

Maggie pondered his words. So he'd gone to help

a friend at an untimely moment in his personal life. That wasn't so bad. "Is there more?"

Too much more, Brady mused. "There'd be a record of a police complaint, too." The frown had returned to her face. "I had a fight with a man in a bar."

"You were arrested?"

Brady rolled a too-tight shoulder muscle. "Not really." Though, he had spent a few hours in jail. He wondered if she was one of those people who saw everything as black-and-white. "I didn't start the fight," he said in his own defense.

"I don't think that matters, does it?"

No, it didn't. All the court would see was a sheet of paper stating that he had been involved in an assault. "It never made it to court because the woman finally appeared and told what happened."

Of course, a woman had been involved. "What does that mean?" Maggie asked, trying to follow him.

"A guy was knocking this woman around. I stopped him. Only the woman took off, so all the police knew was that I had attacked the guy."

"Why did she run off?"

"Loyalty to him."

"But he was hitting her."

"Some women let husbands and boyfriends use them as punching bags. I was lucky. She got courage and came to my defense. One look at her black eye and bruised jaw, and charges against me were dropped." Since those days, he'd been trying to think first, then act.

"Anything else?"

I caused my wife's death. Brady shook his head.

"Well, both of those incidents can be explained," Maggie said more to herself than him. She focused on a bird pecking the ground for food. Like it, in her own way, she was searching for morsels of encouragement to believe she should help him and go through with this scheme. "I want to be certain we understand each other. Our marriage would be a business arrangement. Correct?"

Brady remained tense, though she'd shifted the conversation in the right direction.

"A marriage of convenience," Maggie insisted.

Brady pretended interest in a boy of about twelve in-line skating on the nearby sidewalk. There was one area of this plan he hadn't discussed yet with Maggie, an important one, but he wasn't ready to talk about something that might make her less receptive. "You set the rules."

Satisfied with his answer, Maggie scratched off one problem and went on, "How long will it take for you to petition the court and have Conor living with you again?"

Brady wished he could touch her hand, assure her he would ask no more than necessary from her. "A court representative already checked me out. With you by my side, I could do it quickly. The court will believe I can give Conor the perfect family life."

"Then we can go our separate ways?"

"In a couple of months," he replied. "By then, you'll have accomplished your goal, too."

Maggie knew she needed only to produce a marriage license on her thirtieth birthday. So two months was all the time she needed. But could she leave him then? "We'd need to stay married longer than that."

Almost reluctantly, he nodded. "Yes. It's important everyone believes it's the real thing between us."

Maggie had never shown a lot of courage, never taken risks, been adventurous. She felt weak with the magnitude of her actions. *Wife.* She, who'd never wanted even to consider marriage, would be someone's wife. She, who rarely lied because she did it so poorly, planned to play a game of deceit.

Nerves. Brady saw them in the way she twisted her hands. "It's only for a while."

She wanted to make light of the moment, because she suddenly felt anxiety-stricken. "I should warn you. I don't cook."

His smile came easily now because he sensed her agreement close at hand. "Don't worry about that. I have a housekeeper, cook—" He paused. Irene's position in his life was more complicated than that.

"Oh—that's good." She thought of the maid at her family's home, a gray-haired woman with a thick Yugoslavian accent.

"Renie—Irene. She's a friend."

Maggie heard the trace of affection in his voice. What if his housekeeper looked like Julia Roberts? "She lives in?"

"Yeah, she does."

"Have you told her about your plans with me?" Perhaps that was the real reason he'd asked her to marry him. With her around, he could keep some woman in residence and still escape the wrong image.

"She's on vacation, visiting a sister, but I called her last night."

That clinched it, Maggie decided. An employer didn't discuss his personal life with an employee.

Something more existed between him and the woman. The deception part of their plan bothered her enough. She wasn't certain she could stand being made the fool and talked about behind her back because her husband, even a phony one, had a little cutie on the side. "Is she your—your mistress?"

"Mistress?" He wouldn't laugh. She looked so deadly serious that he knew she would feel insulted if he did. "Renie swears every week she's going to retire."

"She's—she's motherly?"

Brady let his gaze meet hers. She had incredible eyes. "Grandmotherly."

Maggie berated herself. She had to stop jumping to conclusions and needed to be fair to him. "Did you really tell her about this plan?"

"No. I'd rather no one except you and Bennett and me know about it."

"So you told her what?"

"That I'd met someone I was crazy about."

Maggie wondered if her face was crimson. No man had ever said that about her. In her teens, one boy had come close. His words had accompanied adolescent groping in the squeezed quarters of his mother's BMW after a school dance. Perhaps if she'd chosen someone with more finesse, she'd have viewed sex with the same giddiness as her friends. But Curtis Falsworth had cooled her interest in it. She believed sex was overrated. "What did she say?"

"She's pleased."

Maggie was great at thinking of problems. "If she lives in, won't it be difficult to fool her?"

He grinned wryly, admiring her intelligence and the

way she analyzed everything. "If you're willing, I think we can make everyone believe this is the real thing. For the next week we need to be together a lot." He searched his mind, recalling he had one out-of-town trip at the end of the week. Four days open between games and interviews to play the smitten fool. "What do you like to do?"

Maggie sent him a questioning look, unsure if she should take his words to mean what they sounded like.

"Do you like to watch baseball?"

Maggie shook her head.

"Football?"

"No. I've never seen a game."

"You've *never* seen a game?" He found the idea impossible, until he remembered Kirsten saying something similar. Football wasn't part of the curriculum or social activities of a girl who'd attended finishing school. "What about hockey?"

Maggie simply gave him a tight-lipped smile. Judging by the enigmatic expression crossing his face, she deduced he'd never known anyone who didn't like sports.

"What do you like to do? If you don't watch sports, what's left?"

Maggie frowned with him. He made it sound as if nothing existed beyond the world of sports. "I play the flute."

Brady did his best to sound hopeful. "I like the flute."

Her smile came quickly at his efforts to find common ground. "I like to read."

"Me, too." He looked genuinely pleased now.

"Uh, I like how-to books, and westerns, and Ian Fleming's James Bond series."

Macho stuff, Maggie mused. "I read biographies."

Brady released a soft, long breath. This arranged agreement might prove harder than he'd expected. Could two people live under the same roof if they didn't talk the same language? "There's a blues club not far from here with a guy who plays the saxophone like—"

"I prefer the ballet."

Brady slanted a you've-got-to-be-kidding look at her. "No ballet."

"Opera?"

He grimaced.

"Theater?"

His head snapped toward her, a trace of a smile brightening his face. "*Damn Yankees* is playing at—"

Maggie shook her head, cutting him short. "I was thinking more about *Death of a Salesman.*"

"Okay, okay." He sat forward, resting his forearms on the table. "You eat. I eat. We'll go out to dinner a lot, let people see us that way. What are your favorite foods?"

Chocolate chip cookies.

"I'm a steak-and-potatoes man."

She would have guessed that.

"Do you like steak?"

"Not particularly."

Brady stretched for patience. The woman wasn't too flexible. "That's all right. I like all kinds of food, lots of foreign foods. Enchiladas and manicotti and moo gai pan, crawfish jambalaya."

Heartburn city, Maggie mused. "I don't care for any of that."

"A hamburger?"

"Yes, occasionally."

He wouldn't give up, he told himself. "Fried chicken?"

"Actually, I'm really more of a semivegetarian."

"By choice?" he asked, looking dumbfounded that anyone would choose to be one.

This made no sense. They couldn't agree on anything. If she chose to be with this man, she would relinquish her tranquil existence. Maggie bounded to a stand. "Maybe this is a mistake."

Brady's heart dropped to his stomach. "It's not a mistake," he insisted, swinging his leg over the bench and moving quickly beside her. "It's going to be fine. We'll go into this with our eyes open. We'll have fun, help each other get what we want, expect nothing else, and when it's over, no one will be hurt."

That sounded as if it would work. Maggie didn't want any promises from him or any man. Promises meant nothing. They were what people used to persuade others, and in the end, they usually broke every promise they made. "You make it sound so easy, but how can it be when we don't agree on anything?" Lightly, he caught her chin and forced her to look up at him. She felt a jolt, and a tingle. Slow-moving, it slithered through her. It annoyed her.

"We don't have to agree on everything for us to enjoy being together," Brady reminded her, trying to keep his mind on their conversation. But her skin felt smoother, softer than he'd imagined. Instead of something convincing and sensible, some reason that would end all her hesitation, he let the words in his mind slip out. ''All I know is that I think you would be a pleasure to be with.''

She was sure she blushed. No man had ever made her do that. Surely he was just being nice. Nothing more. She drew back from his touch. She couldn't let a few soft words have an impact on her. ''I'm really not certain this will work.''

''It will,'' he said with enormous confidence. ''We'll pretend a whirlwind relationship, starting with your dream date.''

That again.

Brady groaned. ''If I have it right, we'll eat at some place that specializes in alfalfa sprouts, then go to the opera. After two weeks of romance, I'll give you an engagement ring, and we'll announce a desperate desire to get married.''

She didn't want to remind him of what seemed so obvious to her. Why would anyone believe Brady McQueen would want to marry Margaret Buchanan?

With a shift of the wind, her scent drifted to him again.

The dampness of rain clung to the air, yet she made him think of a sunny spring day. ''If people think we're hot for each other, they'll believe that.''

Hot! No man had ever been hot for her. Maggie almost laughed. No one would ever believe that. People viewed her as intelligent, not sexy. ''That could be the biggest pretense of all.''

Brady waited until her eyes, blue eyes that made him think of warm summer days, came back to meet his. ''It won't be hard at all, Maggie.''

Chapter Three

She intrigued him, Brady realized. More than he'd expected. He'd spent four evenings in a row with her before he'd hopped a jet yesterday afternoon to cover a basketball game in Seattle. He wondered if she was really so introverted. And if so, why? He reminded himself that he'd failed once at understanding a woman and that had ended tragically. This time would be different.

So what if they'd have only a short-term relationship. For as long as they were together, he would give her the attention he'd failed to give Kirsten.

With time on his hands before the flight home, he dialed a phone number.

Olivia's maid answered with her stiff recitation. "Is Beatrice there?" he asked, referring to Conor's nanny.

"Who's calling?"

She knew damn well who it was. "This is Brady," he answered irritably.

Silence followed, and he wondered how long she would let him hang before she asked Beatrice to bring Conor to the phone so he could say hello to his son. Moments later, Beatrice picked up the receiver.

"Say hello," he heard the nanny prompt Conor.

"Hi." His son's voice warmed him instantly.

"Hi, Conor." Brady pumped up the enthusiasm and brightness in his voice.

"Da."

"Yeah, it's Daddy. What are you doing?"

"Sharks."

Brady laughed. On his last visit, he'd given him a game with a fishing pole and miniature plastic fish to catch. "You're playing with the sharks?"

"Yeah."

"Did you eat yet?" he asked with a glance at his wristwatch.

"Cheez."

"Cheez. Okay." Brady guessed there had been more, but only so much information could be gained from a two-year-old.

"Say goodbye," he heard Beatrice say.

"Bye."

"Yeah, bye. I love you, Conor."

"Uve you. Bye."

Brady clung to the receiver a moment longer. He ached for these phone calls and the sound of his son's voice. Setting down the receiver, he swore. He shouldn't have to beg for a minute here or there with his son. He belonged with him. Convincing the court wouldn't be easy. Olivia could bring up his out-of-town trips. He knew his only hope was Maggie, and the stability she would represent to Conor's life. Both of their lives hinged on a woman who was still a stranger.

Grabbing the telephone receiver again, he punched Bennett's phone number. After soliciting a few details from Maggie's brother, he hit the numbers for the hotel's florist.

With time to herself before she headed to the library for volunteer work at the annual book sale, Maggie drove to her grandfather's home. Though its ownership remained debatable, she'd always tended the garden behind his home since her grandmother's death. She didn't plan to stop until she was told that the house belonged to Cassandra and she was trespassing.

On her knees at the side of the house, she touched the petals of colorful chrysanthemums. She loved flowers, any kind, from the tiny purple alyssums to the elegant prize-winning roses. A few years ago, she'd chosen a bouquet of wildflowers as the subject of a needlepoint she'd entered in a contest, and had won second prize for her small, exact stitches.

Her straw hat in place, she bent to the task at hand as the sun peeked through the mulberry trees and giant willow, dashing the grounds with splashes of light. Weeds had flourished last week because of an unusual two days of heavy rain.

During those days, the charade with Brady had begun.

Attentive, charming, he'd whisked her around

town—lunch at Chez Maurice's, where her cousin and her friends hobnobbed, an evening at the symphony sitting in clear view of Olivia Elliot Scott, dinner at Truffles for the benefit of the newspaper's society columnist who often ate at the restaurant, an afternoon at the horse track, where they sat with one of the owners who was a distant cousin of Olivia's and a member of the same country club as Cassandra.

On the morning of their dream date, a dozen roses were delivered. When Brady arrived that evening, Maggie had questioned where they were going. Brady kept their destination secret, and drove them two hours north to Prescott.

Acquaintances of his ran a bed-and-breakfast on a street lined with Victorian homes. In a private room with an antique fainting couch and wallpaper with cascades of morning glories, she sat at a table with Brady at a large window that overlooked a garden. In costume, his friends served cornish game hens. Maggie decided that the meal definitely surpassed one of waterchestnuts, peas and carrots. After dinner, they drove back to Phoenix to the sight of a sunset ablaze with color, and as Brady had promised they went to the opera.

Maggie had been thrilled and flattered that he'd gone to so much trouble for her when a date hadn't been her reason for bidding on him at the auction. But she prided herself on being more sensible than to get carried away with romantic notions.

Still because she had had fun, she thought some distance from him might help. Fortunately he was out of town. Shuffling forward on her knees, she yanked several weeds, then smoothed the ground with her fingertips. Around her, birds chirped, and a warm October breeze rustled leaves, but it was the sound of a delivery truck's brakes screeching to a halt at the curb that made her raise her head. From her vantage point, she saw the neighbor across the street. Norma Drensen stood at her bay window, craning her neck to see the deliveryman's destination.

No one was more surprised than Maggie when he moved at a clipped pace toward her with an array of blossoms much like those in her needlepoint.

"Margaret Buchanan?"

Maggie simply nodded.

He handed her the bouquet, then whipped his clipboard toward her. "Sign, please."

She smelled the fragrances for a moment. Never had she received flowers before. With the pen in hand, she signed her name. Excitement danced through her. She wanted to ignore it, and couldn't. As the deliveryman hurried away, she brushed one dirty hand on the hip of her worn jeans, then opened the card.

Thinking of you. Brady.

Maggie presumed the flowers were more of his romantic-pursuit strategy. She'd been thrilled, only because he'd touched her soft spot. She was a fool for flowers, but not foolish. The flowers were part of the plan. He'd sent them because they needed to make people believe they'd become enamored with each other. He simply was setting the stage to convince people that what they felt for each other was the real thing.

Maggie ambled toward the house to set the flowers inside. Actually, she wished they'd been delivered at her apartment. Here, she was alone experiencing a first, and she had no one to share her delight with. No one, she mused, with a look around her.

Surely he knew she would be alone, so why had he sent the flowers here? He should have chosen a more public place. The only person who knew she'd gotten them was herself and a nosy neighbor. Why send them to her when no one might know?

Her heart quickened a beat. *To please her?*

Reaching the door, she frowned. Probably not wise thinking. But he'd succeeded. She admired the bouquet for another moment, and she thought of his smile, of the way she'd felt the first time he'd touched her. Maggie, she berated herself, don't be an idiot.

With a look at her wristwatch, she wrapped the flower stems in wet paper towels, locked the door and dug her car keys from her purse. She had exactly one hour and forty-five minutes to get home, clean up, change and drive to the library.

Sliding behind the steering wheel, she started to set the flowers on the car seat, but she sniffed the blossoms again. Pleasure filled her. He had no idea how deeply he'd touched her with the gift of flowers. No idea at all.

Every year the annual book sale took place in the garden courtyard behind the public library. Though the sale had begun only fifteen minutes ago, a crowd of avid readers mulled around tables stacked with this year's donations.

While people meandered between rows of tables stacked with books, Brady remained at a distance, watching Maggie. For the past few moments, she'd carried boxes of the donated books from the library and distributed them on the tables. She looked downright cute in jeans and a T-shirt, with her hair tied back in a fluffy ponytail.

She was no dilettante. But she was enigmatic, he decided.

He saw no bashfulness, no reticence now. With strangers, with people who wouldn't expect any emotional attachment from her, she let her warmth slip out. She smiled at an elderly man, helpfully answered a woman's question about where to find child-care books and laughed easily with another volunteer at the antics of a toddler somersaulting on the nearby grass.

She definitely intrigued him, he admitted again as he pushed away from the tree he'd leaned against since arriving from the airport. He knew little about her and Bennett's background. Men became friends based on the moment and common interests, and passed years together without probing about each other's pasts. Who they were now mattered more.

But to have a relationship with a woman meant understanding where she'd come from, what she felt. He'd finally realized that. Too late. Before any emotional turmoil about Kirsten grabbed hold, he shrugged it aside. This time would be different.

Sidestepping a woman with a shopping bag full of purchased books, he rounded a table at the exact moment that Maggie turned to lift another box of books. "Hi."

Unprepared, Maggie swayed back. She'd have steadied herself in a second, but he caught her waist.

"Sorry." His lips curved. "I didn't mean to surprise you."

That darn smile of his bothered her a lot. Too much. Almost as much as the heat of his fingers on her. Everything is an act, she reminded herself, aware several volunteers were watching them. "Hi," she said with as much ease as she could muster, vowing not to stammer. It was absurd to act like some tongue-tied teenager every time he was near. "I didn't expect to see you—here."

He couldn't help smiling as she nervously tugged at a strand of hair. He wanted to pull her close, tell her to relax. For the first time since Kirsten had died, he felt a need to touch one particular woman. He had no idea why that woman was Maggie, except she was complicated. Even as her sweetness and her spirit appealed to him, he sensed he would peel back layers before he would discover the real Margaret Buchanan. "I called your brother and learned you'd volunteered to help with the sale."

"When did you get back in town?"

"About an hour ago. The flight out of Seattle was delayed because of a rainstorm."

Only an hour ago. She couldn't have gotten the flowers so quickly unless he'd ordered them while still out of town. "Thank you for the flowers." Someone passing behind her nudged her close to him. "Why did you send them?"

"You don't like them?"

The strong male hand at her waist tightened almost protectively as another browser squeezed his way between Maggie and several women halted at the table behind her. Her heart thudding harder, Maggie smelled the clean male scent of him. "What woman doesn't?" she answered in her best nonchalant tone. "Of course I do. They're beautiful. They're—" Again, she was bumped from behind. "We should move," she said, using the crowd as an excuse to step away from his touch.

"Come on this way."

She expected to follow him. Instead, he took her hand in his. Her pulse pounded harder. She'd gone for nearly thirty years avoiding what she viewed as girlish reactions. Get a grip, she railed to herself. "The flowers look like a needlepoint bouquet that I did on a pillow cover."

"I know." Brady watched her closely.

Maggie slipped her hand from his but stilled. "How could you? It's at my grandfather's."

"I asked your brother what flowers you liked, and he described the needlepoint."

A teenager stepped between them to reach around Maggie and pick up a book on a table. "Excuse me."

With a nod, she shifted to give him freedom to peruse all the books. He blocked Brady's view of her and gave her the opportunity to move several tables away to empty another carton.

"That one is good," Brady was saying to the boy. Instead of the slow, unsettling smile he flashed at her, he gave the boy a quick grin.

The teenager gripped the book about the career of Babe Ruth, but his gaze remained on Brady. "Hey, I know you. You're always in the press box at the Suns games."

"What did you think of last night's game?"

"We should have won that one."

"If we hadn't gotten into foul trouble, we would have," Brady said, not unaware of the distance Maggie had put between them.

"Yeah, that's what I thought, too."

Maggie regarded them over a box of books. For another minute, he carried on a conversation with the boy as if they were old friends. Head bent, she dug into the carton. She'd always envied people who had such easy rapport with everyone. She supposed that was why he was good at his job. He could walk in anywhere and talk to anyone with the same confident poise.

"Where were we?"

She didn't need to look up. Brady hunkered down on the opposite side of the box. She knew it was foolish to put so much emphasis on the flowers, but she disliked puzzles of any kind. "I'm surprised my brother remembered that needlepoint pillow I did." She nearly stuttered as he ran a finger along the inside of her wrist. Why was he pushing so much closeness today? Tingling from his touch, she rose. So did he.

"When I asked him about your favorite flowers, he remembered it."

He was confusing her, going beyond what was expected.

"He said you'd be gardening at your grandfather's this morning. Every Tuesday and Thursday between seven and nine."

How boring she sounded.

"I thought you'd like them."

That he'd meant to please her baffled her more. Why hadn't he simply bought a dozen roses, a token gift that she could ignore? "This doesn't make sense. Why did you send them?"

He stared expectantly at her, then grinned again.

"What I'm getting at," Maggie insisted softly, "is that it makes no sense for you to send me flowers. That isn't really part of the plan."

"Why can't it be?"

"Because no one will see them."

"Except you."

"Yes, me." Her voice trailed off as he brought his face inches from hers. Then he kissed her. His mouth moved lightly, briefly over hers.

Startled, she started to jerk back. At the last second, she checked herself. Around them, several acquaintances stared inquisitively. Brady's words echoed in her mind. People needed to think they were crazy—hot—for each other.

Flushed, she looked adorable to Brady, and even more tempting with such surprised confusion on her face. "You could pretend that you enjoyed it," he whispered against her lips about a kiss he'd been contemplating for days.

Oh, how she wished she hadn't.

"Talk about something." He thought one of them needed to keep everything looking normal. His hand no longer framing her face, he gave her the space she wanted. "We're supposed to be whispering sweet nothings to each other."

"What?"

"Come on, Maggie." Amusement gleamed in his eyes. "Play the game. Do you like watching the Three Stooges?"

"I—I never have."

"Never?" he asked softly.

"Brady, why are you here?" She willed herself to talk about something more substantial, and stop thinking about the feel of his warm hand on her.

"I came because I learned you have a fund-raiser party to attend tonight. What time should I pick you up?"

"I wasn't going to stay." She'd planned only to make an appearance, then leave after thanking the necessary people for their contributions.

"Now you can. We'll go and mingle."

"But I don't—"

"Maggie, we have to start convincing people."

With a look down, she frowned. She'd never expected so many complications when she'd agreed to this plan. "Yes, I suppose we do have to convince them it makes sense that we might soon get married," she said, her words as much an affirmation to herself as to him.

"No."

Her head jerked up. His voice had sounded soft, seductive, sexy.

"We have to convince them that we're falling in love." He watched her eyes widen before he turned away. "I'll pick you up at seven," he called back.

Maybe she'd acted rashly when she'd agreed to this marriage bargain, Maggie reflected later while dressing. It went against everything she'd planned for herself. After too many disappointments in her youth, by her twelfth birthday, she'd stopped disillusioning herself and believing marriage and happily-ever-after went hand-in-hand. By the time she'd turned seventeen, she'd made a decision. She liked her single life-style. No marriage and no entanglements meant no heartache.

So why was she primping so much for an evening with him? Sure she found him attractive, but if this was to be truly a business deal, such thinking could only cause her trouble.

Standing before her closet, she viewed her evening wear and frowned. Hardly a social butterfly, she owned two serviceable dresses. A navy blue dress with a white collar and cuffs and the black dress with a high round neck and long sleeves that he'd seen at the bachelor auction. To complete the ensemble, she usually added a string of pearls and her practical, chunky-heeled pumps. But if she was dressed like someone's maiden aunt at this evening's gala event, no one would believe any man, especially Brady, would be so totally infatuated with her that he would propose after only weeks of dating.

Scowling, Maggie nudged clothes along the closet pole and scrutinized each outfit. A minute later, she dashed out the door.

She let the saleswoman at a nearby exclusive boutique talk her into a black silk dress with spaghetti straps. At home, she dug out diamond earrings that had belonged to her grandmother. With the ring of the doorbell, she surveyed herself one more time in a mirror near the door, then opened it. "I'll be one more minute," she said, instead of a greeting and rushed to the closet for her jacket.

Before she'd slipped one arm in, he stood behind her. The brush of his hands on her bare arms made her tense. They'd lingered longer than necessary. She was sure of that. "Thank you."

"You're welcome," he replied. Her face glowed, her eyes looked bluer. Only one thought came to mind. She looked stunning. Why hadn't he noticed before just how really beautiful she was? "You look lovely," he said softly when her stare came back to his.

Maggie mentally groaned. She'd wished for him to say something like that to her, but she hadn't expected him to say it with such sincerity, to be so convincing. "That was nice of you," she answered, determined to remain unaffected.

"No, it's the truth, Maggie."

Because she didn't know what to say, she turned away from his gaze.

Accurate observing and analyzing came with Brady's job.

The first time he'd entered the soft, rose-colored living room days ago, he'd thought it charming and feminine. He'd decided then that she wasn't as cool as she wanted people to believe. Maggie Buchanan was hiding a very romantic nature.

Flanked by some of the city's finest estates, the hotel chosen for the benefit offered a view of Camelback Mountain. White mini lights graced the shrubbery that lined the curving drive. Inside, people lingered near the lobby's floor-to-ceiling windows, with a view of a manicured lawn and flower gardens.

Stepping into the ballroom with its high ceiling and sparkling chandeliers, Maggie spotted her best friend.

Tall and painfully thin, Deidre Hensworth motioned to them.

"A friend of yours?" Brady asked, bending his head toward Maggie's.

Deidre was too good of a friend to lie to, but what choice did she have? Maggie dreaded the inevitable exchange. "I've known her since boarding school."

As Brady eased her jacket from her shoulders, he considered her last comment. She'd grown up in the cold, often pretentious world he'd wanted to save his son from. Although boarding school was probably on Olivia's agenda, he wanted Conor to be with him, relaxed and happy. He visualized the two of them sprawled on the living room floor, watching a baseball game on television. He wanted to take his son bowling. He wanted to fix him breakfast in the morning, let him live within walking distance of school, eat dinner with him every night. He wanted Conor to feel loved.

"The man beside her is Henry Quinten III. She's madly in love with him."

Beneath his hands, her bare shoulders felt fragile. "Is *he* with her?"

"He's—" Her voice faltered as his warm hand slipped low to touch the small of her back. "He's an entomologist, too involved with his microscope and slides to notice her that way, though they are friends."

Brady scanned the sea of faces. There were women who were more beautiful than her in the room, but he would have noticed her first, a natural porcelain beauty with fair skin, blue eyes and rich raven tresses that were swept away from her face and held in place with a decorative comb.

He'd heard her laugh once, when Bennett had suggested this scheme. He hadn't forgotten the warmth that he'd heard in her soft, smoky-sounding laugh. He'd yet to hear it again, but planned to. "We should join them, shouldn't we?"

Maggie wondered where his mind had wandered during the past few seconds. "Yes."

"Act one begins," he said in a low voice, for only her to hear.

Maggie understood his comment. During all the previous dates, they'd kept to themselves, but tonight meant performance time. She was absolutely certain she would never pull this off. On a long, steadying breath, she led him toward Deidre and Henry standing near the floor-to-ceiling windows and their view of the immaculately landscaped lawns.

With his hand against the small of her back, Brady felt it straighten as if someone had poked her. She was a breath away from denying everything they'd planned. "She'll understand later," he assured her.

Maggie cast him a quizzical look, amazed he'd been so perceptive of her concern. "I hope so."

"If she's a good friend, she will."

Clinging to what he'd said, Maggie plastered a smile on her face while she made introductions. She didn't miss Deidre's wide-eyed awe when Brady flashed his hundred-watt smile at her.

"You don't belong to the National Historical Preservation Society, do you?" Henry asked. His tux fit poorly on his small shoulders and thin frame.

"Brady's a sports columnist with the *Herald,*"

Maggie replied. They stared in puzzlement at her. She didn't need psychic ability to know they believed that Brady was hardly her type.

Henry's eyebrows rose with his frown.

Didn't he realize that not everyone could be a sportswriter? In fact, few people were talented and lucky enough to secure such a job.

"How did you meet?" Henry asked as his puzzlement knitted his brow.

His question made sense to Maggie. She'd always limited her social contacts to the historical society, the library and an animal rights group. "We met at a bachelor auction."

Henry gaped; Deidre appeared stunned. The Maggie they knew didn't waste time on such frivolous activities. The bachelor auction was one of the charity affairs they all usually skipped.

"I know Bennett," Brady said to fill the silence.

They both nodded as if that made more sense.

"So you're not interested in history?" Henry asked.

What could he say? Brady wondered, and shook his head.

Like Maggie, her friends were the serious, studious type, and the truth would make him sound like an academic nitwit. In his teens, he'd lived his life for after-school practices on the field.

This plan was crazy, Maggie reflected. Beside her, Brady had slipped into conversation about the Chicago Bulls with two of the fund-raiser's contributors.

Meanwhile, Henry droned on about an espresso shop near the library. "I counted forty-one different flavors of coffee beans."

"Interesting," Maggie managed to reply, determined to veil her boredom.

Brady saved her from listening to Henry listing all of them. Moving his hand to her waist, he waited for Henry to take a breath, then recommended, "Let's get something to eat, Maggie."

She grabbed at a way to escape Henry's rambling. "You know this is ridiculous," she said for Brady's ears only. "None of this will ever work."

Nodding a greeting in passing at the owner of the city's basketball team, Brady steered her toward the buffet table and snagged a mushroom stuffed with something green. "What won't?"

"Us. We're too different," Maggie insisted.

"There's no problem." A smile curved the edges of his lips. "Opposites attract."

Maggie grew more determined to make her point. "Or clash." Maggie chose a shrimp. "And we're not really—"

He brushed his knuckles along her cheek. "Sh. Someone is heading our way."

She traced his stare and groaned. Who that someone was made her stomach knot. "My cousin."

"Interrogation time?"

"Afraid so."

"Relax," he said soothingly. "She seems so curious that she can't get here fast enough."

Maggie winced as she watched her cousin wind her way quickly around others to reach her.

All glamour and glitter, Cassandra was dressed in purple crepe. "Margaret," she said in her usual between-the-teeth delivery. "You look—"

"Stunning," Brady finished for her. Fragile, even

vulnerable, he mused. He wasn't a man used to ut-tering compliments to a woman, and she wasn't a woman who expected to hear them, but he wished he could tell her how the sight of her when she'd opened the door for him had snatched the breath from him.

Her cousin's eyes darted to him. "Who—who...?"

"Who are you?" Anderson asked, finishing his wife's question while he looked over the top of his thick-lensed glasses at Brady.

Maggie thought they sounded like a pair of owls. Meeting her cousin's stare squarely, she made the in-troduction.

"How did you meet?" Cassandra asked in her drill sergeant's voice.

"Bennett introduced us. And—"

"It was one of those where-have-you-been-all-my-life moments," Brady piped in, his arm tight at Maggie's waist, drawing her closer, his lips pressing against the softness of her hair.

"How convenient," Cassandra quipped.

Maggie had geared herself for this moment. "I beg your pardon?"

"That you've suddenly got a man in your life."

"Yes, how lucky I am," she said, and beamed up at Brady, copying Michelle Pfeiffer's adoring gaze at one of her screen lovers.

Cassandra made a sour face. "I'm going to be ill." She turned in a huff, followed by a shell-shocked-looking Anderson.

"I don't believe it," he mumbled as he fell into step beside his wife.

"Charming pair," Brady murmured.

"You heard him," Maggie whispered. "They didn't believe us."

"They will."

He'd sounded so certain. How could anyone be so sure of himself?

"You've been quiet ever since we left," Brady said when they stepped from the elevator in her apartment building. "Worried about the cousin?"

Head bent, Maggie fished in her purse for her keys. "A little."

"Don't assume you'll lose the house."

"It's hard to think positively when I haven't been for months," she admitted while unlocking the door. "I was weeks from my thirtieth birthday and not intending to marry."

Brady considered how little Bennett had told him about his sister. "Why not?"

"Didn't Bennett tell you?"

He bent his head closer to hers and touched several soft dark strands that had sprung loose from the tight restraint of the jeweled comb. "Tell me what?"

"I don't believe in love."

She'd hinted at that the night they'd met, but he'd never heard anyone actually say that before, and she'd delivered the statement in the same emotionless tone someone might use to declare, "Thank you, but I don't want another cup of coffee." Though curious, he kept his questions to himself. "Then I'm offering you a perfect solution."

"I suppose so," Maggie said, more relaxed now than she'd been all evening.

"Maggie?" He waited until she had finished fiddling with the keys and dropped them back into the small purse, then he leaned toward her.

"What?" His face was close, so was his mouth, and she was suddenly all nerves again. "What are you doing?"

"I'm going to kiss you." He planned a friendly one that he believed would stop the tension between them. They needed to feel comfortable with each other.

"What?"

"Kiss you," he repeated softly.

Pure panic raced through her as he slowly angled his head and his mouth hovered near. She shouldn't do this. If she kissed him, he might guess she'd thought about it. "Why are you going to?"

He chuckled softly. "You're going to damage my ego. I'm going to kiss you now so you'll feel comfortable doing it in front of others."

"You expect us to kiss again in front of others?"

At that moment, it occurred to him that Margaret Buchanan was even more innocent than he'd believed. "Makes sense."

Not to her. How could they stay emotionally uninvolved if they included kissing in their relationship? "What makes sense?"

Brady brought his mouth a hairbreadth from hers. "I love you."

Maggie reared back. "What?"

"That's what we're trying to convey," Brady reminded her. "I love you. You love me. Right?"

"Pretend love," she murmured, nodding, unable to take her eyes off his smiling mouth.

"People in love do kiss." Lightly, Brady ran a fingertip along the line of her jaw. He'd planned a slow, undemanding kiss, one that would convey a message of friendship. He planned on patience, tenderness. He'd thought the best thing they could do was get the kiss out of the way.

Then the warmth of her lips was beneath his. Passion. He tasted it in her sweet mouth, felt it in the way her body swayed into his, heard it in her soft, barely audible sigh. It occurred to him that he wasn't totally in control. He tightened his hands on her shoulders as he slipped under the desire churning through him. He never expected her kiss to spark passion within him. He'd kissed and walked away from more sophisticated, more seductive women. Was it her gentleness and innocence that made him feel the same excitement that he'd known his first time?

Maggie had been certain she would feel nothing. She'd dated others and had felt nothing. Yet she was straining against him. Dazed, she felt a twinge of panic as a multitude of sensations swarmed through her along with an ache of womanly desire that could break through her protective wall.

Eyes closed, she placed her hands against his chest, but couldn't push him away. His lips pressed down harder, parting her mouth with a practiced touch, moving slowly as if savoring her taste. In a mindless haze, caught up in a craving, she melted into him. She didn't want it to be this way. But he shattered her composure.

Why of all the men she knew was Brady scattering her good sense? This was a business arrangement, nothing more. And yet, even as his mouth left hers to caress her jaw, she yearned for his lips on hers again.

As he drew back, she told herself she had to be alone, needed time to think. And they needed ground rules. She couldn't get caught up in any fantasy. She knew better. She never would believe in happily-ever-after. "I thought..." she said, still breathless. It was time to set him straight, past time. "I thought we'd agreed. No hanky-panky."

Brady couldn't help it. He laughed. "What an expression."

"Whatever you want to call it," Maggie insisted. "This marriage is a business deal."

After a kiss like that, he doubted either of them would remember that, but she was right. This was temporary. They both wanted no involvement. Stepping back, he removed his hands from her. "I can't promise 'hands off.'"

"Because we have to convince others," she said so softly he strained to hear her.

"Yeah. To convince others," he murmured before turning away. And he had to convince himself that he wouldn't want to do that again.

Chapter Four

A curious Deidre called at seven the next morning. Behind Maggie, the toaster popped. Cradling the phone between her jaw and shoulder, she lifted the English muffin from the slots.

"Tell me everything."

If only she could.

"He's utterly fab-u-lous-looking," Deidre purred in Maggie's ear.

"Yes, he is," Maggie agreed. Despite raised eyebrows and whispers behind their backs, were people believing that Brady McQueen, Mr. Eligible, was bonkers about the quiet, reserved Margaret Buchanan?

"Maggie, I'm so happy for you. I'd heard gossip that you'd bid for a date with him, but I hadn't believed it until I saw you with him last night."

If her best friend believed, it suddenly seemed possible others might.

"Really. I'm thrilled for you. Finally there's a man in your life."

"Yes." She truly hated that she couldn't be truthful to her friend.

"You looked beautiful last night."

Maggie couldn't help smiling. He'd sort of said that, too.

"This is so wonderful. You always have been so—so reclusive."

Her friend's tact stirred her smile.

"You'll tell me more at brunch tomorrow, won't you?"

Maggie buttered her muffin. How would she get through a face-to-face meeting with Deidre and not be truthful? If Deidre asked a lot of questions, what would she do? She hardly knew Brady. He'd spent years with another woman, had had a child with her. Vaguely, Maggie recalled Kirsten as a delicate blonde whom men had admired. She wasn't anything like Kirsten. Yet when Brady had kissed her, she'd felt as if anything was possible.

Unconsciously, she pressed her fingertips to her lips. If she closed her eyes, she could conjure up the feel and taste of his kiss, the way his lips had angled over hers, the heat of them, the touch of his tongue.

Deidre's excited tone cut through her reverie. "Maggie, is it serious?" she repeated.

Maggie made a frantic link with reality. This was insane.

"Maggie, is it?"

At times she'd felt lonely, wished for a special man

in her life, but hadn't her mother thought that way, too? And look at the heartache she'd faced. "It could be." She was amazed at how easily the lie flowed from her lips.

"That would be so fantastic for you," Deidre said excitedly. "I know how important your grandfather's house is to you."

"Yes, it is," Maggie answered. It was, she recalled, the only reason why she'd agreed to this plan in the first place.

Brady had jogged before dawn. Besides exercise, the morning run usually provided moments alone to unclutter his mind. Not this morning. Maggie was beginning to drive him crazy. He'd seen her in plain duds with her hair tied up tight, reminding him of a spinster schoolteacher. He'd seen her in jeans and a T-shirt with a ponytail swinging, looking a decade younger. He'd seen her dazzling in that black dress that bared her shoulders and clung to her hips. He'd seen her stutter, nervous as a schoolgirl, he'd been mesmerized listening to her converse as an equal with a biochemist at the benefit, and he'd felt admiration when she'd stood with her chin ready for a punch during that confrontation with her cousin. Intelligent, beautiful, sensitive.

He couldn't stop thinking about her. Why? Because of one kiss? That made no sense. He'd kissed his share of women, he understood desire and had always been able to control it. In fact, he'd cooled his personal life since he'd begun his custody pursuit. Maybe that was the problem. It had been a while since he'd been with a woman. To play his part, he couldn't avoid touching her in public. For the plan to succeed, they needed to look head over heels in love with each other.

Oh, hell. All of the reasoning fell flat. The familiar tightening in his gut when she'd opened the door last night warned him that he wasn't thinking of her as only a business partner. She'd looked beautiful. He'd wanted to kiss her, and, damn, he had no right thinking about her that way. He'd hurt one woman. The last thing he ever wanted to do was hurt another. There was just one *but*. And it was a big one. He wanted to see her.

By midmorning, he stood beside his car and viewed the Victorian-style house that meant so much to her. It was painted a Wedgwood blue, with white window frames and lacy porch spindles. He viewed the steep, irregular-shaped roofs, the imposing tower and a cutaway bay meant for rubbernecking by the occupants. The porch spanned part of the front and looked suitable for sitting on and for sharing conversation with neighbors.

As he started up the steps, the sound of Elvis Presley wailing ''Love Me Tender'' drifted to him. He'd thought Maggie would be here this morning, but he couldn't picture her as an Elvis fan. He'd called Bennett earlier, and he'd told him that she'd left a message on his answering machine. At nine this morning, she was going to their grandfather's house. Though Bennett had been right when he'd told him about the flowers, he'd apparently struck out this time.

Brady climbed the last step to the porch. Whoever was inside might know where to find her. He rang the doorbell, heard nothing, then knocked on the door.

But he was lousy at waiting. Certain someone was inside, he opened the door and stepped in.

The furniture was dusty, the result of the house being vacant since her grandfather's death. Instead of calling out, he wandered in the direction of the music. The king of rock 'n' roll was pleading "Don't Be Cruel."

Brady reached the kitchen doorway and stopped in midstride. The prim Margaret Buchanan stood at the kitchen counter, her hips swaying, her bare feet moving. He knew then that he was sunk.

Beneath the reserved propriety lived someone who possessed the capacity to let loose and have fun. Enjoying himself for another moment, he braced a shoulder against the doorjamb. He'd have waited until the song ended, only she turned and jumped at the sight of him.

"Sorry."

Her one hand to her chest, Maggie swept an arm back and flipped off a cassette player. "What are you doing here?"

"You like Presley?"

No one knew that except Bennett. "Yes."

It took Brady more effort to keep a straight face when he spotted the tamale wrappers in the garbage can and the opened box of chocolate chip cookies on the table. Who are you, Maggie? he wondered, not for the first time.

She kept her backside glued to the kitchen counter as an odd twinge of pleasure coursed through her at seeing him. "Would you like something to drink?" Despite her mother's other failings, she had trained her daughter to play the perfect hostess. "Coffee or…?"

Brady dragged his gaze from her bare feet and the toenails painted a bright red. "Coffee." He stepped into the room and jammed his hand into his pocket to keep himself from reaching for her.

"How did you know I was here?"

"Bennett." Brady studied the kitchen's long, narrow windows. "It's an interesting house."

"It's a Queen Anne style." Maggie rushed her words to quell her nervousness. "The design was popular in the last two decades of the nineteenth century."

She spoke with such seriousness. "It's got a great porch," he said.

"Yes. The gingerbread ornamentation is finely crafted."

He really didn't know what she was talking about.

"It's one of very few Victorian homes in the state. Some places like Colorado have many different styles, especially Greek Revival. Those are the ones with columns. And Gothic Revival designs look like the old abbeys and castles of England with their steep-pitched roofs and pointed-arch windows."

Probably she would feel as lost as he was if he started talking about a forward pass to the tight end, or one man out, a man on first and the winning run on third. They lived in different worlds. He'd already tried to blend into her world with another woman and had failed. Despite their efforts, he and Kirsten had never blended. Her life had bored him, and she'd been apathetic to his. She'd never gone to a game with him or—

Thoughts stopped. On the kitchen table, the newspaper was folded to his column. During the four years he'd been married to Kirsten, she'd never read his column.

Maggie saw where his gaze had wandered. "I thought I should read it."

God, he felt like grinning like an idiot. "What did you think of it?"

"You're a good writer. Interesting," Maggie said honestly. "But—" she paused. "But what does poke check mean?"

"It's hockey lingo. It's when a defensive player uses his stick to knock the puck away from his opponent's stick." Brady smiled as her brows drew inward. "Was that the only thing you didn't understand?"

"No, but—" Maggie shrugged. She would require some kind of sheet with terms on it to fully understand everything he'd written.

"You need to see a game."

She wasn't certain she wanted to. "It must be rewarding to see your words in print."

"For a bestselling author, probably." He gave her that million-dollar smile. "But it's hard to get a big head when you know that most people use your printed words to line birdcages, housebreak dogs or throw potato peelings on."

Maggie looked away to veil a smile.

"It's a sports gossip column," he said self-deprecatingly.

She gave him his due. "It's more than that. It's insightful."

The compliment pleased him. Standing near, he inhaled the subtle lemon scent in her hair. He wanted to touch the soft, dark strands. No, dammit, he wanted to bury his hand in them. All that unfamiliar analyzing he'd done earlier went to hell with her so near. Beneath that prim, neat facade, she hid a woman with a unique sense of humor, one who kissed with a passion that promised warmth—heat.

"Why did you come looking for me?"

Shoving a hand into his jacket pocket, he eyed the peeled plaster near the back door. The moment ahead promised to be filled with tension. "To give you this," he said, and opened a ring box.

Maggie stopped breathing. Nothing had prepared her for this. Diamonds glittered and winked at her.

Small, Brady knew. Someone with her money could buy a ring twice that size. "If you don't like it..."

"It's lovely." Like a wedding, an engagement ring had never entered her mind. She drew a breath, trying to regain her composure. "I never expected this." Never. wanted ties to any man. Some people bonded, kept promises better than others. But those people weren't in her family.

"I thought it would make everything appear more official." Actually, he couldn't imagine marrying her and not giving her an engagement ring first. In his mind, it symbolized a promise, if not to love forever, then to cherish always. And he would do just that. For without her, he would never be able to get Conor. "I don't think you realize how grateful I am that you're willing to do this."

Mechanically they moved closer. She held out her hand; he slipped the ring on her finger.

Brady watched the light go out of her eyes. Though her lips still curved in a smile, she hid something painful behind it. He wondered if she'd secretly harbored some romantic dream of the moment when she got an engagement ring. "I know this is short notice, but I'd like to get married by next weekend."

"Next weekend?"

"It has to be fast, Maggie. I don't want to give Olivia more time with Conor."

She watched him nudge back the cuff of his windbreaker to check his watch. Now that he'd done what he'd planned, was he impatient to leave?

Brady witnessed a transformation. A seriousness in her eyes dulled their color, hid their beauty. Every time he was with her, he felt more determined to see them smiling. When they did, he felt warm, warmer than he'd been since before Kirsten died. Some time alone might help him sort through what he was feeling. Enjoy the temporary arrangement, he told himself, and quit overanalyzing everything. "If I give you until seven tonight, can you finish here and spiff up for dinner out?"

"Dinner?" A celebration for their engagement? As quickly as the thought formed, Maggie shook it away.

"Can you?"

"Yes, I'll be ready." He simply wanted to go out to show off the ring, to make sure everyone knew about the engagement. It was a prop for their performance. Nothing more. She'd learned long ago that the mind provided a better barometer for judging relationships. She would be a fool to believe in the fantasy that was beginning. And she was no fool.

But he did make it difficult to remember that. He'd

been kind and attentive. Mostly, he'd made her feel special.

That evening, Maggie sat across from him in an exquisite and overpriced restaurant with a view of the city. Its clientele came from the upper crust of society who claimed ancestors from the *Mayflower* or the American Revolution. Judging by the stares directed at them, she assumed many of the customers knew Brady and maybe Olivia. "Was this a favorite restaurant of yours and Kirsten's?" she asked, looking away from the wall of windows and the moon slipping behind a cloud.

Brady watched her gaze sweep the room again. He could have told her that he'd never liked this restaurant with its heavy gold drapes, gilt-framed paintings and overstuffed brocade chairs. In the background, a cellist performed highbrow music meant to force whispered conversations. "Kirsten liked it."

"But you never did?"

"Never." He hung out at a sports restaurant near the newspaper offices where the hamburgers were juicy and the beer was ice cold and the customers watched games on big-screen television sets.

Maggie toyed with the thin stem of her wineglass. "How did you and Kirsten meet?"

"Kirsten and I should never have happened," he said in response to her previous question. Then she would be alive now. "Fate does control our lives," he added almost philosophically. "In high school, I barely passed classes. I didn't think I needed to bother. I had my life figured out. I was going to play football." He caught her puzzled frown and grinned over the top of the wineglass at her. "Bet you can't understand that kind of thinking, can you? Did you spend every spare moment in the library?"

"I always buried my nose in books." All kinds, Maggie mused. They offered her an easy way to escape some dreadful moments in her own life.

"I only opened one out of necessity," he admitted. "I was sure I didn't need to know all that." He shrugged. "Dumb. Dumb thinking. But that's how it was back then, and I did win a football scholarship to college. Then fate stepped in and laughed at me. An injury forced me to reevaluate my life and ended my hopes for a pro football career. That's when I began knuckling down to studies, and I chose journalism."

He'd lost a dream, Maggie realized.

Except for his first semester, he'd been a straight-A student. "If I couldn't play sports, I decided I could write about them. The first job I got was with a small local newspaper. Kirsten came in one day to place an ad for a Junior League Christmas sale. They were selling homemade crafts and Christmas decorations. I bumped into her because I wasn't watching where I was going. I was reading the race track results."

Maggie smiled with him. "Was it love at first sight?"

He thought the question an odd one from her. "I didn't think you believed in that."

"I don't." Maggie smoothed the napkin on her lap. "But other people do. I thought you might be one of them."

Brady waited for her to raise her head, for her eyes to meet his again. "Why?"

"Because you're—" She paused, unsure how to be honest and not insult him.

He laughed as if aware she was hedging. "What? What aren't you saying?"

"You excite easily," she answered. During the drive to the restaurant, he'd flicked on the radio, tuned in a football game and had cheered unexpectedly, giving the steering wheel a hearty bang with both hands. Maggie had sat quietly, a little unsure how to react.

Brady didn't need an explanation from her. She'd looked at him as if he'd grown two heads when he'd reacted to the radio news of the home team's touchdown. He chuckled softly, but the sound was so out of place among the reserved clientele that several people glanced their way. "Yeah, I do." Actually, Olivia had used the word *crass* to describe him.

"Why was what you heard on the radio so exciting?"

"A sixty-five-yard run is exciting."

"Is it?"

"Maggie, you need to go to a football game." If nothing else, he'd teach her how to have fun. "Do you spend all your time volunteering?"

"Mostly. I volunteer a lot of time to the Animal Humane Society and the Wildlife Association. And I help at Pioneer Village to give tours to visitors." She looked up as the waiter materialized to refill their water goblets. "You never answered my question. Was it love at first sight with your wife?"

Actually, he'd been dodging conversation about Kirsten.

"Not exactly. When we met again, I was working for the *Herald*. She came to the newspaper office to meet her great-aunt there. She was on the newspaper's board of directors.'' He stared at her pale, delicate hand resting on the table and slid his fingers over it. Part of the act, he told himself. He was supposed to look enchanted with her. That was getting easier with every minute they spent together. Considering the roles they had to play, he supposed that was good. They would be more convincing if they lusted a little for each other.

Maggie couldn't say when it had started feeling so right to be touched by him. ''Was that when you started dating her?''

''She knew I wasn't what her mother would view as suitable for Kirsten Elliot Scott. In fact, Olivia threatened to disown Kirsten when she found out we were seeing each other. Kirsten kept seeing me, but her mother's approval did matter. Before we married, I signed a prenuptial agreement. If our marriage ended, which was something Olivia was sure would happen, then I got nothing.''

Maggie thought about her own wealth. She'd inherited a remarkable sum from her grandfather.

''You don't have to be concerned. I'll sign one with you before we get married. Since the marriage will be one of convenience, and temporary, it's the right thing to do. Anyway, there is money in trust for Conor. He's entitled to it as Olivia's only grandchild.''

''I wonder what stipulation she's put into the trust.''

''Thinking about yourself and what your grandfather did?''

"My grandfather left me the money. It was the house he put in trust."

He smiled wide, amused. "That still doesn't make sense."

"Oh, it does," Maggie said as she resumed eating. "He knew that was all that really mattered to me."

"Yet he made it difficult for you to get it."

"He wanted me to have it under his terms. He believed marriage would bring me happiness."

"You don't?"

"Happily-ever-afters belong in fairy tales."

He studied her. She'd spoken lightly, but he'd heard an underlying sadness in her voice. For some reason, she had a pessimistic view about marriage. He wished again he'd asked Bennett more about their family, but guys didn't probe, didn't ask. Bennett had told him that his father was deceased and his mother lived in Spain. In time, Brady planned to find out more. "You had an odd grandfather, but I think I would have liked him."

"He would have liked you," Maggie said with certainty.

"Would he?"

"Yes, you're spontaneous."

Brady chuckled quietly. "You make that sound great. But I believe most people refer to me as impulsive." He didn't view it as a bad trait, but he would guess the thoughtful, patient woman across from him with her structured life would. "So except for Bennett, he was your only relative?"

"Well, there is Cassandra."

After she'd recovered from the shock of seeing him with Maggie, Maggie's cousin had drilled Brady with a look that would have bored a hole through a lesser man. "Guess you never went to that fund-raiser with a date before."

"No, never. I'm usually on the committee that plans that evening, so I'm always too busy."

Making sure other people have fun, Brady deduced.

Maggie couldn't recall Bennett ever mentioning anything about Brady's family. "Don't you have any relatives?"

"Not here. After my father retired, my parents made a trip to Florida, and liked it, so they moved there. Because my sister was working in real estate, it was easy for her to join them. I come from a middle-class background. Comfortable, but nothing like yours.

"They all liked it in Florida, wanted me to join them, but I hated the humidity. What about you? I never asked Bennett too much about his family. Does your mother ever live here?"

"She stays in Europe." Always had.

Brady felt as if a door had been slammed in his face.

"I talked to Bennett earlier. He told me that he's already petitioned the court to let you have custody of your son after the wedding and until a final hearing."

"Yeah." Brady let the joy he'd felt earlier during Bennett's phone call fill him again. "That was great news." To prevent her from distancing herself from him again, he went on. "About the wedding. We could have a small reception. Invite a few friends to the wedding. Bennett said he would have it at his apartment." Brady wished he knew what she was thinking. "I realize my problem is more complicated than yours."

Maggie poked her fork at the last asparagus spear on her plate. "I knew that."

"Good." In his whole life, he'd never tiptoed so much with any woman. Well, that wasn't entirely true. Rebecca Lewis had tied him in knots, too. But at thirteen, he could be forgiven for acting like a stumbling jerk. "The problem with your house will probably take longer than my custody battle with Olivia, unless she keeps trying."

Obviously, he was already anticipating the time when they could end this farce.

Brady stalled for a moment, not sure how to bring up another subject. Dive right in, McQueen, he berated himself. "About the honeymoon."

Her head shot up. "Honeymoon?" Her stomach fluttered.

"With us getting Conor right away, we can't go on one."

"I—I didn't expect one."

Well, that cleared that up quickly, Brady mused.

"After all, this is a marriage in name only."

His eyes pinned her. "No, it won't be."

"What?"

"Sh," he murmured, aware some curious looks had turned their way.

Maggie drew one long, deep breath. "I think I'm misunderstanding you."

"No, you're not."

He gave her one of those grins that heated her skin. "I thought you understood, Maggie."

"Understood what?"

"I'll be your husband." He hunched across the table to bring his face closer to hers, to speak softer. "The marriage has to be authentic, for real." He saw shock widen her eyes and felt uneasiness churning his own stomach. She couldn't back out now. Please, God, don't let her back out. He needed her desperately.

Maggie opened her mouth, but for a long moment, her voice refused to work. "Why?"

"Because everyone needs to believe this wasn't done for ulterior motives."

"How could they possibly know?"

Brady released a long breath. "Because you would tell them."

Maggie was totally confused now. "No, I wouldn't. Why would I do that after I agreed to get married so we both could get what we wanted?"

"Because you're too honest," he said quietly, trying to smile despite the worry that kept fluttering through him. "Aren't you honest?"

"Yes, I am."

"Ever tell a lie?"

She sat back in her seat for a moment and tried to recall one before she'd agreed to this.

With her silence, he went on, "That's what I meant. You're an honest woman," he said with admiration, realizing he liked that about her.

"But I wouldn't have to lie about us. We would be married."

He repeated her words. "In name only. But that might not be good enough for me to keep Conor."

Maggie couldn't eat another bite. She set down her fork and stared at the glittering diamond on her finger.

She hadn't counted on this complication. She wasn't certain that she could separate love and passion. What if she lost herself to him, let herself believe in love just because he held her against him, he touched her and excited her, he made her feel like his woman?

"In a custody hearing, you could be asked if we—"

"Consummated the marriage," she finished for him.

Brady couldn't help smiling. "Made love."

"Sex is not love," Maggie countered, as much as a reminder to herself as him.

Brady watched her nervously touch the ring. "Sometimes it's part of it."

Maggie saw no point in arguing with him. "Believe what you want."

He wished he understood her better. But he was already striking zero on that ability. If he'd understood women, Kirsten might still be alive. "Would you lie?"

"No," she admitted without hesitation.

"Then this would all have been a futile effort. There is only one way to guarantee that we both win. So what is it? Yes or no."

How had her orderly, tranquil life become so off kilter? "I have to think about that." What had she gotten herself into? she wondered.

Chapter Five

She couldn't go through with this marriage, Maggie decided before ten the next morning. Her common sense told her this was nonsense. She'd viewed the marriage as a business merger, nothing more, but if they made love—had sex, she corrected herself—pleasure might tip them away from a controlled strategy.

That wouldn't do.

Brady promised to provide a complication she didn't want in her life. And she knew how important control was. For too many years, she'd seen her mother's lack of it.

Done with breakfast and her morning exercise time, she whisked out of her apartment for her weekly brunch with Deidre. After it, she would call Brady and tell him she was sorry but she was bowing out.

"I've been dying to hear everything." Deidre indicated no interest in the Belgian waffle on the plate in front of her. "Tell me about that," she said with curious enthusiasm and touched the sparkling ring on Maggie's finger as if it were as delicate as a rose petal. "He's certainly a different type for you."

A twinge of disloyalty nagged at Maggie for not telling Deidre the truth about Brady. But earlier this morning, before she'd left to meet Deidre for brunch, Bennett had warned her that for the plan to succeed, she and Brady needed to keep it a secret. Before Maggie had a chance to tell him she'd decided against it, he'd ended the conversation. "I guess that's why I found him so interesting." She poked her fork into the fruit flan to sample it, then returned her attention to her omelette. "Because he is different from the others I've dated. And once we started talking, we found we had similar interests." *Please don't ask what they are,* Maggie prayed.

Deidre daintily took a bite of her waffle. "This engagement is kind of quick...unexpected, isn't it?"

Would doubts flourish even after the marriage? "You don't like him?" she asked, because it sounded like a logical question one friend would ask another.

"He's gorgeous. However, you have always told me that you never intended to get serious about anyone."

"Meeting the right person changes one's viewpoint." She'd generalized her response so she wouldn't have to lie. But this all seemed so deceitful to her. However, until she leveled with Brady, she felt honor-bound to continue with their plan.

"It must have," Deidre said, drawing Maggie's attention back to her. Uncharacteristically, her friend set an elbow on the table and hunched forward. "Everyone is talking about you two. I mean, really, you can't be seen so often with a man and not expect people to believe that you're having a meaningful relationship with him. But that..." Her voice was filled with the same high-pitched excitement it had contained when she'd first seen the ring. "Engaged. You," she added, as if it were some kind of incredible feat. "Are you planning a long engagement?"

"Ms. Buchanan?" Saving her from answering, the waiter appeared beside her and bent forward slightly. "A phone call for you."

"For me?" Maggie stared at the portable phone he'd brought to their table. With a soft thank-you to him, she offered a greeting to the caller.

"Morning," Brady's voice sang.

"How—" She wanted to ask him how he knew where to find her, but was aware of Deidre's close scrutiny. "Brady, how wonderful to hear from you so early."

"Deidre's listening, huh?"

"Yes." Maggie offered Deidre her most I'm-so-ecstatic smile.

"To the question you didn't ask. I knew where you were because you have brunch with Deidre Hensworth every Friday."

Oddly, until he'd entered her life, she hadn't been aware that what she'd viewed as a structured, carefully scheduled life sounded disturbingly boring and predictable.

"This is my day with Conor," Brady said, bringing

her attention back to him. "I'd like you to come with us, since you'll be a part of his life for a while."

Again the object of Deidre's stare, she maintained a light, airy tone. "I'd love to. Where will we go?"

"A picnic. There's a park nearby."

It sounded so family-oriented. "Wonderful." Alone with him, she could explain her misgivings about the marriage. Brady told her a time when he would pick her up, then said goodbye.

"You're so lucky," Deidre gushed. "Everything is so wonderful."

"Everything," Maggie murmured.

Brady felt tied in knots as he strolled to the bathroom for a shower. He planned to view Maggie as a friend, one who was helping him out of a jam. Sure he was attracted to her. Lusted for her. He liked being with her, but involvement with another woman was a risk, and he didn't take chances anymore. Yet he was asking her to take plenty of them, wasn't he?

He recalled how stunned she'd looked when he'd made the suggestion about a wedding night. He'd had little choice. One night. He needed one night with her. But what if she backed out now because of what he'd said?

Letting the water run over him, he tried to relax, but he wondered if by the end of the day, Maggie would stop everything and all his hopes for his son being with him would be over.

By the time he picked her up, a bright sun hung high in the sky. Tension lingered in him with her silence during the drive past stately homes to Olivia's house. She'd yet to mention *the* problem, and he couldn't deal with it now. Any time with Olivia required all his attention.

When they turned onto the driveway, Maggie sat straighter. Before he'd arrived, she'd decided to wait until after he picked up his son to announce her decision. So now, Act II began, she mused while she perused the palatial home with the massive white pillars. "It's an imposing house."

Brady braked his car in the driveway, flicked off the ignition and prepared for battle. "So is its owner." With a shrug, he yanked out the keys, then opened his car door. He'd never come to Olivia's home and felt relaxed. "Don't expect pleasantries."

Maggie opened her door to join him on the steps. During a short period of her childhood, she'd lived in a similar palatial house with her parents. Did footsteps echo in this house, too? Did a coldness exist even in rooms flooded with warm sunlight?

Brady raised the brass knocker and banged it against the heavy door.

Within seconds, the butler stood grim-faced before them. "Good morning, sir."

"I'm here to pick up Conor." Not waiting for the butler to admit them, Brady grabbed Maggie's hand and strode past the butler and into the foyer.

"Please remain here. I'll announce your arrival."

As the butler stepped away, Brady murmured, "Igor."

His tension reaching her, Maggie offered him a slim smile and settled gingerly on a Louis XIV chair. She felt no more comfortable than he did in this house. It was too formal, austere, unwelcoming, a mausoleum. It was ostentatiously decorated in marble, mirrors, gilt and velvet. A staircase led to a stained glass window, drew the eye to the ceiling with its Gothic motifs in green, gold and silver and the gilt chandelier.

As quietly as he'd left, the butler reappeared. "Please come this way."

Brady kept her hand tight in his. "I hate this damn drawing room," he said in a low voice.

The double doors opened to a room with a gilt-bronze chandelier, the shaft of which carried golden cherubs that resembled Cupid. Similar ones were carved into the white Italian marble mantelpiece. Even the settee and chairs had cherub figures for the arm supports. Swags of flowers painted on the wall were duplicated in the carpet. *Moneyed, lavish* and *vulgar* described it best.

On one of the chairs, a stern-looking, white-haired woman, the epitome of the society matron, angled a look of disdain Brady's way. "I've been informed that you brought a guest with you," she said, unaware of Maggie, who was lingering by the door. "If you think I will tolerate my grandson being under her influence, then you—" Her voice trailed off as she spotted Maggie.

Brady considered the impression Maggie offered in the blue blazer and white blouse buttoned all the way to the base of her throat. No way could Olivia find fault with her. "This is Margaret Buchanan."

Olivia's sharp eyes narrowed. "Buchanan." She let the name roll off her tongue. "Lilith Buchanan's daughter?"

Brady darted a look from one woman to the other. What was happening here?

The moment Olivia had mentioned her mother's name, Maggie had felt a resurgence of the shame she'd known as a child. Throughout her youth, there had been whispers about her mother.

"Where's Conor?" Later, Brady planned to find out why the mention of her mother's name had made Maggie go pale.

"Upstairs, of course," Olivia replied, regaining some of her supercilious tone. "He's with the nanny."

"I'll go get him," he said to Maggie.

She felt the reassuring squeeze of his hand on hers before he turned away.

Olivia's voice remained as cool as her eyes. "I can only assume you are your mother's daughter or you wouldn't be involved with such a man."

Maggie didn't miss the slight. She wouldn't even refer to Brady by his name. "Your daughter married him," Maggie reminded her, feeling defensive for Brady.

"Over my objections, she chose to marry him." For the second time in seconds, her pinched face tightened with a frown. "Is that an engagement ring?"

Maggie realized that unconsciously she'd been holding her hand behind her back until that moment.

"You're going to marry him?" Olivia tapped her cane on the floor with her agitation. "Yes, it would seem you are like your mother."

Maggie had no intentions of playing her punching bag. "Who I am isn't important."

"I believe you are wrong about that. The court might think differently." She sent Maggie another haughty stare. "Do you really think the courts would have given me custody of his son if he was an acceptable influence?"

Words Maggie intended to say remained silent as Olivia's comment sent her mind in a different direction. She had barely questioned Brady about why he'd lost custody of Conor.

"I have custody of Conor because Brady is unfit to be his guardian."

It was her tone that made Maggie's stomach somersault. What if Brady didn't deserve to be helped in getting Conor back?

"If he plans a distressing court battle, I can make it all very unpleasant—for both of you. Remind him of that."

As they drove away from the house, Maggie couldn't forget her words. Several times, she glanced back at Conor in his car seat. Why had Brady lost his son? He'd claimed that he'd been lost in grief for months after Kirsten had died. Had he been telling the truth? Would Bennett have suggested this alliance between her and Brady if he hadn't believed Brady and his son belonged together?

Braking at a red light, Brady checked his son in the rearview mirror. When he'd entered the nursery, Conor had thrown himself at Brady's legs. An ache, one that had knotted his throat, had nearly unmanned him as he'd felt his son's small arms tight around his neck, clinging when he took him from the nursery.

Not quite two years old, he wasn't totally aware of what was happening in his life. But being absent from his son's life five out of seven days a week left Brady with an unbearable emptiness.

He couldn't stop thinking about Conor. It wasn't hard to gather what was happening during the hours they were apart. A nanny fed and dressed him, put him to bed. Olivia didn't give a damn about Conor. He was too young, too much of a nuisance at this age. She was waiting, leaving his needs to an employee until he was of an age when she could mold him into a submissive child who would operate like a robot and do what she wanted. "What did Olivia say?" he asked, because Maggie had been quiet, too quiet.

"She believes she'll win in a custody battle."

"I can't let that happen."

Maggie swiveled a look back at Conor. He was the image of his father, same color hair, same infectious grin.

"It feels so good to have him near. I thought I was going to lose him," he admitted, saying his biggest fear aloud now because it seemed less likely. "She has the power to gain permanent custody of Conor."

Maggie stared out the window at the passing scenery of wide-open land sprinkled with desert vegetation, prickly totem pole cacti and some stragglylooking desert bushes of pale green foliage, and in the far distance, the hazy outline of steep buttes. "Where are we going?"

Brady pulled away from his thoughts. "To my place. I thought you might like to see it since you'll be living there for a while."

Maggie opened her mouth to tell him she'd changed her mind, but Brady went on.

"I know you have a lot of commitments in the city. If living this far out is a problem—"

"How far is it?"

"City limits."

She noted he'd driven from the freeway to a paved highway.

"It's at the next turn."

If she weren't going to call this quits, Maggie would have viewed where he lived as no real problem. She could have driven the freeway into the city. It wouldn't take more than half an hour.

In an upscale desert subdivision of stucco homes, he wheeled the car onto a paved driveway. While she stood beside the car, Brady unhooked Conor from his car seat.

"Come on," Brady urged, holding his son.

Maggie followed and stepped into the living-dining room with its highly polished, honey-colored oak floors and wood-paneled walls of the same shade. A big upholstered hunter green sofa and matching chairs conveyed a sense of quiet refuge.

"The kitchen's this way," Brady said, after giving her time to take in her fill of the living room.

Maggie trailed him. Simple pole chairs with woven backs and seats, bright Navajo-designed rugs and a gable-ceilinged dining room with a river rock fireplace emphasized the western motif.

"What do you think of it?"

She released the same smoky-sounding laugh that had rocked him before. "I love it."

"You don't find it too desolate?"

"It's not that far away from the city."

Setting Conor on the floor, he realized that he'd expected her to hate it; Kirsten had. With a gleeful laugh, Conor rushed to a wooden toy box in the corner and lifted the lid to dig out his favorite toy.

"Did you have this house built?"

"No, it belonged to an architect whose wife wanted to return to Cape Cod." Brady motioned with his head toward the refrigerator while he filled the coffeemaker. "See if there's anything in there to take along on our picnic."

Maggie scrutinized the contents in the refrigerator. "I don't know what this is."

He winced at the casserole dish in her hands. "An experiment that should have been tossed out a week ago. Put it back. I'll dump it tomorrow. You said you don't cook?"

"Do microwave meals count?"

Brady chuckled. "Not really."

"Then the answer is no." She didn't want to admit that throughout her childhood she'd entered the kitchen only twice, once to sneak food for a stray dog, and the other time to talk to the cook. Both times her mother had reprimanded her for, as her mother had said, sitting like a philistine at the kitchen table. Maggie had never entered the kitchen again.

"Coffee's almost done." The coffeepot hissed.

Zooming a car under the table, Conor peeked out. "Eat."

Brady reached down for him. "Hungry, huh?"

"Ya. Eat."

Smiling, he lifted Conor up to sit on a chair.

Maggie had already seen a difference in Brady's son. When she'd first met Conor, he'd been shy, clinging to his father; now he was smiling and laughing. And Maggie allowed gut instinct to lead her. She knew Olivia was wrong. Conor belonged with his daddy.

"Adrin?" Conor asked.

Maggie sent a questioning look at Brady. "What does he want?"

Was she having second thoughts? Brady wondered. "A drink," he answered. Marriage to him included instant motherhood.

"Adrin," Conor repeated more emphatically.

After a detour to the sink for a drink of water, they drove to a grocery store near the house. Brady talked to everyone—the produce man, the grandmother ahead of him in the grocery checkout line, the adolescent bagging groceries.

Shortly after, they arrived at the park and set out their picnic on a blanket that Brady had provided. She really didn't know him, Maggie reflected while she ate a slice of cheese. His life-style was so different from hers. She'd never been on a picnic, especially as a child. Was this what families did? she wondered as she watched Conor run with short steps a few feet away, drawn to a butterfly.

"Bufy," he yelled out, his arms raised as he tried to catch it.

Brady relaxed his back against a tree trunk and stretched out his legs. "I never asked. How do you feel about kids?"

She had nothing against children. In fact, she liked them. It was marriage she had no use for. Yet, when she'd agreed to this marriage bargain, she realized now that she'd been agreeing to be mother to his child. She hadn't considered that, either. "Brady, we need to talk." She had to end this now before she lost all control of the situation. Looking down, she packed the remains of their lunch and set it in the picnic basket. The sharp, distinct aroma of Brie mingled with the sweet fragrance of Chablis.

"Is this about Conor?"

The concern in his voice made her look up. "Brady, he's adorable."

She liked his son. For some reason, that assurance was enough for him. He regarded her over the wineglass in his hand. "Olivia told you I don't deserve him, didn't she?"

Maggie watched a pained look flicker across his face.

"I understand her bitterness toward me. She blames me for letting her daughter down."

Maggie swore she heard guilt in his voice, but what did he have to feel guilty about? "Will you explain?"

"I should have known what Kirsten was feeling. I should have known what she was doing, but I was too involved in what was happening in my own life." More times than he could count, he'd relived the days before Kirsten's death. She hadn't looked sad. She would smile, make love with him. He hadn't any clue she was so unhappy. He'd never suspected. And that was what he couldn't forgive himself for.

Maggie sensed he'd wandered somewhere private.

"I should have paid closer attention to her wants, but when we had Conor, I was happy. I thought she was, too." Brady rubbed two fingers at a spot between his brows. "Because of my job, I was out of town a lot. I guess she felt that I was neglecting her. I never meant to."

Maggie sat still, certain he was talking more to himself than her.

"Before Kirsten's death, she told me she didn't want to live at that house anymore. We were going to sell it and move closer to the city." He'd never told anyone this before, but he realized she deserved explanations. "I think what it really was about was her mother. She didn't know how to break free of Olivia's hold. It was as if she didn't trust any of her own decisions."

Having been with Olivia even for a few moments, Maggie sensed the autocratic atmosphere Kirsten had grown up in.

"I don't think I was any better for Kirsten than Olivia had been. The marriage was shaky," he said between sips of the wine. "I couldn't live with her incessant need for her mother's approval. It seemed more important to her than anything else." *And he hadn't understood.* She'd seemed so confident, but she'd needed constant reassurances that she was loved. "On the night she died, I had to fly to Philadelphia to interview a baseball player." He recalled the excitement in the sports world at that time for the young player who'd broken a batting record.

"You weren't home then?"

"No, I wasn't. Usually when I was out of town, Kirsten stayed at Olivia's. Like I said, she didn't like being alone." He avoided Maggie's eyes. "She drove there, put Conor to bed and made a drastic mistake. She mixed some prescribed drugs with alcohol, then went swimming."

Maggie's heart lurched. She hadn't known. She

doubted few people outside of the immediate family had ever been told anything except that Kirsten McQueen had gone swimming alone and drowned. "What kind of prescription?"

"At the funeral, I asked her doctor. He told me it was for depression."

"Was she on medication all the time?"

"It seems she was." He felt the tightening in his chest that he'd dealt with for months after Kirsten had died. "I didn't know it. That's pretty lame, isn't it? A husband should know what his wife is doing."

"It must have been a shock for you to learn that."

"She hid that from me." He shook his head. "Why, I don't know."

Maggie yearned for the right words. "I can see why you were grieving, feeling so lost."

"It wasn't grief," he admitted. Sadness clouded her eyes for *him,* he realized. Without touching him, she caressed something within him. "It was guilt. If I had paid more attention to her, been a better husband, I might have prevented her death."

Maggie touched his hand. "You can't blame yourself for what someone else does."

How could he not? He'd failed Kirsten. "After the accident, I couldn't get away from the guilt. I was out of it, mentally lost for a long time. Olivia wasn't. She went on as if nothing had happened. That's when she petitioned the court for temporary custody of Conor."

"How old was he then?"

"Thirteen months." Brady went on as if she wasn't there.

"When I snapped back to normal a few months

later, Olivia said she was keeping him, so I went to your brother to help me get Conor back.''

Maggie was at a loss for words of comfort, something wise that would ease the misery he harbored within him.

Brady balled a napkin. Talking about that time hadn't helped. Nothing might ever alleviate the blame he felt. Looking up, he glanced at Conor, then scrambled to his feet as Conor reached for a wasp on an oleander bush. ''Conor, no!''

Like a doe caught in the headlights of a car, Conor froze, his blue eyes widening. The wail began instantly.

Brady winced. He'd meant to protect him from a sting, not startle him. ''Come on, big guy,'' Brady soothed, and drew him into his arms. Tears still flowed down his son's round cheeks.

Though unsure how to help, Maggie had followed Brady to his son. ''We could get an ice cream,'' she suggested while she ran a hand over the back of Conor's head. ''You like ice cream, don't you?''

His eyes sparkling with tears, he nodded. ''Ic-cream.'' With the same quickness that the tears had started, they ended.

Who are you? Brady wondered again, having caught a glimpse of something she would insist didn't exist—a nurturing ability. ''Thanks. He's the most important person in my life,'' he said fiercely.

No longer startled, as if he'd received his cue, Conor reeled around and plunged at his father, yelling, ''Down.''

Laughing, Brady fell back to the ground, with his strong arms wrapped around his son. In return, Conor growled, pretending to be a lion. His father growled back and gently rolled Conor with him first one way and then the other.

If Maggie had had any doubts, they disappeared at that moment as she heard Conor's laughter, saw his father's smile, watched this strong man's gentle care with his child while they played their imaginary game.

She couldn't call this off, not now. The house meant a great deal to her, more than others might understand. The happiest days of her life had been when she'd lived in it with her grandparents. But Brady had more at stake. She'd experienced the heartache of custody battles after her parents had divorced. She knew they resulted in one casualty—the child.

Though his son was too young to understand, unless Brady regained full custody once and for all, Olivia could repeatedly file for guardianship of the boy. And whatever Maggie had to do to help him, she would do. "Brady?" She waited until he'd straightened and Conor had shifted his interest to the ants on a nearby sidewalk. "We'll get him back." The smile Brady returned made her want to cry.

On the edge of emotions she didn't fully understand, she turned away to grab the picnic basket. She'd already stepped over a self-imposed line. Already she was feeling emotional ties drawing her to Conor. Maternal instincts emerging? Perhaps. What she felt for the boy seemed explainable. He was still a baby, caught up in something that could in time make his life miserable.

What was her excuse about Brady? She'd always

kept herself detached from others, why couldn't she with him? She didn't believe in promises, yet because of him and his love for his son, hadn't she already made one?

Chapter Six

Plans began.

Before Brady had hopped on a plane to Houston two days ago, following the basketball team on a road trip to Houston and then Miami, he had spent an hour at the airport with Maggie scribbling names. He'd given her the job of picking out the invitations. Getting something done in an impossibly short amount of time came easily to her. She prided herself on efficiency, on good time management.

Within two hours after he'd left town, she'd chosen invitations and had contacted an engraver who was known for doing rush jobs. That evening, she'd addressed envelopes and slapped stamps on them. The wedding invitations had been in the mail within twenty-four hours after Brady had left town.

Two days later, while at a meeting of the Historical Preservation Society, Maggie learned the guests had received their invitations.

As Henry led a discussion about adding an old theater building to the National Historical Register, Deidre oohed about how pretty the invitation was. In an excited manner, she slid from one topic to the next without taking a breath. "Do you have a dress yet?" she whispered.

Maggie shook her head. Henry had already sent a scolding look their way because of their whispers. "I have time," she answered her friend.

"Not a lot." Deidre's concern about the wedding details had become more intense since Maggie had asked her to be her maid of honor. "How many guests?" she questioned out of the corner of her mouth.

"About forty." Maggie had hoped for a more private wedding, but Bennett had insisted they needed to have some kind of public celebration.

"The building meets the criteria," Henry was saying. "It's over fifty years old." He shuffled papers on the highly glossed conference table in an office that a local law firm allowed the society to use to hold their meetings.

"I'm sure Abraham Lincoln attended something there," Henry's rather ditsy sister said.

"No, he didn't," someone else countered.

"What kind of flowers?" Deidre questioned.

Maggie whispered back. "I haven't thought about that yet."

Her friend frowned.

Head bent, Maggie fingered a corner of the newspaper in front of her that she'd opened to Brady's column.

Henry's sister insisted, "The building needs to be associated with a historically prominent person."

"No, it doesn't," Deidre piped in, referring to the nineteenth-century building that had been built in the Romanesque Revival style. Henry smiled with pleasure at her for finally diving into the discussion. "It simply has to possess distinctive aesthetic characteristics."

Maggie let her mind wander. She and Brady hadn't discussed again the topic of them having a real marriage, which really meant sex. In her mind, real marriages included more, such as sharing innermost thoughts. That didn't mean she hadn't pondered what it would be like sleeping beside him, his hands touching her, passion in his eyes. Or what it would be like to feel his body beside her every night, to wake up with him every morning. What bothered her most stemmed from one fact. Since she'd never been the type to swoon over terrific looks and masculine physiques, though he had both, why did she, who'd always been so sensible and in control, feel an edgy kind of anticipation when she thought about that?

"If its cultural worth is proclaimed," Deidre added, "we can get support to preserve it, and they won't tear it down. Isn't that true, Maggie?"

"What?" Maggie glanced around the table. All eyes were on her. She supposed she wasn't acting normal, but she felt bored with their mumblings and was anxious to leave.

A slim, knowing smile tugged up the corners of Deidre's mouth. "So we must get it listed with the

National Historical Register,'' she said, not even waiting for Maggie's response.

She had to stop thinking so much about Brady, Maggie berated herself. Flaking paint, a broken window, holes in the pantry floor all needed attention at her grandfather's house. As soon as the meeting ended, she would go there.

She caught Henry's concluding comment about talking to the city council, and rose before the others. She needed to be busy. Sitting allowed her too much time to think. For the first time in her life, she didn't want to consider her actions or their consequences.

Inside the elevator, she grew impatient. The last person she wanted to see was Anderson, a possibility since his investment company's offices were in the building.

Instead of Anderson, she stood face-to-face with Cassandra as she stepped outside.

Her cousin glided away from the Mercedes parked at the curb. ''I heard.'' Icy disbelief laced her voice.

When her eyes drifted to Maggie's finger and the engagement ring, Maggie nearly hid her hand, like a child caught pilfering a cookie. Brady was right. Her honesty could be their downfall. Deceiving people proved close to impossible for her.

''I never thought you capable,'' Cassandra said with a cursory glance at the engagement ring.

She had to pull this off. Maggie had sensed the restrictive environment Conor was living in with Olivia. He needed the laughter, the love his father could give him. ''I beg your pardon,'' she said, hoping for a smidgeon of thespian talent.

''Oh, so sweet, so innocent. You know what I'm

talking about. You've done something to get a man in your life." She studied Maggie for a long moment, her eyes narrowing to slits. "You're paying him, aren't you? That could be the only conceivable explanation. Men like Brady McQueen don't get enchanted with women like you."

Of course they didn't.

Maggie saw a flicker of revelation flare in her cousin's eyes. "Just a minute. Oh, my, this is—" She released a mirthless laugh. "Brady McQueen," she said thoughtfully. "He was married to Kirsten Elliot Scott, wasn't he?"

Maggie's stomach knotted instinctively. Their social circle was smaller than she'd imagined.

At Maggie's silence, Cassandra's head inclined only slightly, her brow lifting in a way that had always amazed Maggie. She wondered how people learned to control an eyebrow.

"There was a child. Now, let me think for a moment,"

Cassandra murmured with a look up at the sky as if a message were written there for her. "A boy." Her eyes slanted at Maggie. "A boy who lives with his grandmother." A slow, too-knowing smile curved the corners of her lips. "He wants his son back, doesn't he?"

Maggie felt sick.

"He thinks marriage to you, the saintly Margaret, will convince the judge that he can provide a better home for his child than Olivia Elliot Scott." She sort of laughed. "Does he really think he can win against her?"

Maggie let her ramble on. Lawyers always warned

their clients in criminal cases to keep their mouths shut. She thought that advice wise for her, too.

"I can hardly wait for the wedding. It's soon, I understand."

Gossipers loved sudden news. Maggie imagined she'd become the topic of interest since wedding invitations had been received. At her cousin's expectant look, Maggie had no choice except to respond. "Yes, soon."

Cassandra wagged a long-nailed finger at Maggie as if she were a small child. "Pure Margaret isn't so lily white, is she."

Maggie felt her spine sag as Cassandra sauntered past her. Instead of going to the house, she needed to see Brady, fast.

Common sense had warned her this plan wouldn't work. This was all such a mess. Why did she ever think that someone as cunning and shrewd as Cassandra would accept without question her plans to marry? Of course she would interpret it as a last-ditch effort to beat the stipulation in the trust so Maggie could keep the house.

Uneasy, she drove toward the newspaper office. With luck, Brady was back in town.

He was, but he wasn't at the office. A barrel-chested man with a bald head sucked enthusiastically on the end of his fat cigar as he approached Maggie. His twinkling dark eyes peered over the rims of his glasses at her. "You're Maggie, aren't you? The name's Charlie." He offered her a pudgy hand. "That's quite a rock he sprung for," he said while he stared at the ring. "When he returns from a trip, he usually works at home." He gave her a strange look as if she should know that. "He faxed his column in to the newspaper about an hour ago." He turned those eyes back to his computer screen. "So he sure won't be coming here."

"Okay. Thank you," Maggie said quickly, aware that meant another half an hour while she drove to Brady's house while her nerves intensified and worries escalated.

"Tell him he won the bet," Charlie called out to her.

Maggie paused in midstride. "The bet?"

"Howsier is helping carve pumpkins."

"Pumpkins?"

"For the children's hospital party. Every year the newspaper has a coffee-and-cake thing in the cafeteria. It's volunteer work."

"Howsier will help," she repeated. Receiving his nod, she headed for the exit.

She had a lot more to tell him.

Maggie drove faster than usual before she became aware of the speedometer. Immediately she eased her foot from the accelerator. If she started acting uncharacteristically, wasn't that like a forewarning that they should back away from this plan? Because of the conversation with Cassandra, Maggie already had proof that this wouldn't go smoothly.

Pulling into Brady's driveway, she wondered if she should have called first. He'd just flown home. He could be napping or working. She shouldn't have come.

Despite the thought, she'd already climbed the steps and was at the door. She knocked once, then heard noise at the back of the house and retraced her steps.

They could still forget their plan. They hadn't gone too far to stop, she reminded herself while she crossed the uneven ground of small stones to reach the backyard. That's when she stopped dead in her tracks.

A private paradise existed, with lush tropical landscaping and a pool that blended into the shrubbery, which seemed to fade into the distant mountains.

Standing in the glow of sunlight, Brady was stripped to the waist, his snug jeans riding low on lean hips. Bronzed, muscled, his skin gleamed with a light film of sweat. Feet firmly planted, he dug dirt from a hole in a steady, effortless motion.

As she went toward him, he turned. Maggie only allowed herself a glance at the hair on his chest, the clearly defined muscles cording his stomach, the fine line of hair that disappeared beneath the waistband of his jeans.

"Hey, this is a surprise."

She wanted to blurt out her doubts about the bargain they'd made, but he kept grinning at her as if everything was right in the world. How wrong he was, Maggie reflected. "I have a message for you. Howsier will help carve pumpkins."

He cracked a smile. "I'll be damned."

"Is that good news?" she asked with a tinge of annoyance, because she thought the sky was falling and he kept grinning about something as inconsequential as making faces on pumpkins.

"Howsier is the newspaper's general manager. I made a bet with Charlie that I'd get Howsier to carve this year."

"How did you do that?"

It hadn't been easy. Howsier St. Claire came from the same pompous mold as Olivia and Maggie's cousin. "In return, I agreed to play Santa Claus this year for the employees' Christmas party."

"Why was that so important?"

"He likes getting the upper hand on employees. He thinks I think I'm too macho to ho-ho for the kids."

The man had no idea who Brady McQueen was. She'd seen him with his son. He loved kids. All parents said they loved their children, but she could tell that Brady genuinely liked being with his son.

Tossing the shovel aside, Brady strode toward her. When she'd arrived, troubled thoughts had etched that faint line between her brows again. Now a smile lingered on her face. Reaching out with a fingertip, he traced the curve of the smile. "That's nice."

With effort, Maggie held still beneath his touch.

"You looked so serious."

She didn't return his quick grin. "We have a problem."

"You forgot to add someone to the invitation list?"

Maggie shook her head, wishing their problem was something as simple as the wedding arrangements.

"Okay." He noted the small frown line had returned between her brows. "You can't get a dress?"

"I can get one." She hadn't bothered to look yet, probably wouldn't now.

"The hotel overbooked, and we can't hold the reception there?"

One of them needed to show an ounce of common sense. "I don't see how we can go through with this. My cousin guessed our intentions."

Brady wasn't surprised. Since neither her cousin nor his ex-mother-in-law were dummies, he'd calculated for this possibility. He wiped the back of his hand across his sweating brow. "Come on in. I'll give you a glass of iced tea and you can tell me what happened."

Maggie followed him toward the door.

On the way, he snatched up his T-shirt from a nearby bush, then tugged it over his head.

In the kitchen, Maggie gave an account of her meeting with Cassandra while he took out a pitcher of iced tea and poured two glasses.

"She can guess all she wants." He placed the glass in front of her before he straddled an adjacent chair. "That doesn't mean anyone will know anything."

She wasn't convinced.

"Don't worry so, Maggie." He realized he wanted to kiss her. He realized, too, that he'd missed her. Instead of moving close, he leaned away from her. "We'll pull this off."

"How? Cassandra will try to prove the marriage was arranged."

"She won't be able to."

"How can you be so sure?"

"How can anyone prove we don't love each other? Sure, it might seem like a coincidence this happened before you turned thirty, but that's all she can prove."

He made everything sound so easy.

"What's the problem with you and the cousin?" Brady asked, certain it began in childhood.

"She thought she was better than me."

No, she didn't, Brady mused. She felt threatened by Maggie. Perhaps she saw the confidence and intelligence in Maggie that she lacked. "Why did she think that?"

Maggie felt him inching too close to everything she'd tried to forget for years. "Her mother was my aunt, my mother's sister. They never got along." She shrugged. "I suppose the animosity passed on to the next generation."

"Do you feel animosity toward your cousin?"

"Not really," Maggie said truthfully. "But if someone doesn't like you, you give up trying to be friends with them."

"Why didn't your mother and her sister get along?"

Maggie curled her fingers around the iced tea glass. "My mother stole a boyfriend from my aunt, the man she was engaged to."

Brady released a low whistle. "Kind of heavy duty."

"Yes, and she never forgave my mother." Enough, Maggie decided. She didn't want to keep talking about the past. "What about your parents?"

The door had shut again, Brady knew. "What about them?"

"Did you tell them yet about the wedding?"

"Yeah. I called them last night and told them I got engaged and when the wedding is. They're thrilled."

"Didn't they wonder that it was so sudden?"

"They're used to me doing things impulsively."

So he was living up to his reputation. People would believe him; she was the one who would stir doubts. Margaret Buchanan never did anything on the spur of the moment.

Brady watched her nervously push back strands of

her hair. "The wedding will be a good excuse for them to see Conor. They adore him."

So did he. Before seeing him with Conor, she'd pegged him as a reckless, undependable man. Then she'd seen the responsible man who'd been with Conor.

"Do you want to go to a game with me tonight?"

"You could tell me when there's a poke check," she said, recalling the hockey term.

He smiled slightly. "That's hockey. This is a basketball game."

Ridiculously, she felt a quickening of her heart when he'd asked her. She allowed the excitement for only a second. He was asking her to go with him for one reason only. "Either way, it would be a public appearance. We need to be seen."

Brady suddenly wanted to shake her. "Forget the damn bargain we made. I want you to go with me. I'm asking you to go because I want to be with you." He bridged the distance between them, and in a slow stroke, he ran a fingertip across her cheek. "Now, do you want to go out with me?"

She could barely register what he'd said. Was he going to kiss her again? It would only complicate the situation. No, she wouldn't let this get out of hand, she promised herself.

"Maggie?"

Uneasy, not with him, but with feelings inside her, she pushed to her feet. "I need to leave."

"Not yet," he said, standing, too.

His hand curled at the back of her neck, holding her still. His breath floated over her face before his lips warmed hers.

Gently he nipped at the corner of her mouth.

Instead of pulling away, Maggie swayed toward him. It was his gentleness that seduced her. She would never be able to resist it, not now, not later. And later there would be more kisses, she knew; she hoped.

Already her head spun. Heat racing through her, she answered his kiss on a soft moan, her tongue meeting and challenging his. A longing stirred within her. She sighed again, touched his face, deepened the kiss. And she knew, too, something that had never happened before with any man was going to happen with him. She would make love with him willingly.

Pressed close, her breasts flattened against his chest, she clung a moment longer. Only a moment. Even breathless and feeling a little dazed, she vowed to remain sensible. If she kept her feet firmly planted, this affair with him would be something she would remember fondly long after it was over.

It took effort, but Brady became aware of her stiffening in his embrace, and he pulled back. For now, he would be satisfied with the warmth of her kiss lingering on his mouth. "Maggie, do you want to go?"

"Yes," she answered, still breathless. And knew she was agreeing to more than this evening's date.

They arrived at America West Arena before the crowd started drifting in.

Seated in the press box on Brady's lap, Conor swayed to the "Star-Spangled Banner." He clapped his hands and yelled with the crowd while happily munching on a cookie that Maggie had provided. Before the first quarter ended, he was sleeping in Maggie's arms.

Brady punched in some notes on the computer. "If he gets too heavy, give him back."

"He's not too heavy." Maggie stared down at Conor's innocent face, and lightly she smoothed back hair from his forehead. She supposed that was how her parents had felt. When she'd been too much trouble, they'd sent her away.

"Four thousand twenty points," someone said in the row of seats behind Maggie.

Cuddling Conor close, she cast a glance at the man with the bulbous nose and head of white hair. "Four thousand twenty-nine," she said in response to his comment to another man.

"Naw."

"She's right," the other man called out from three computers away. "Wilt Chamberlain scored that many in eighty games while with the Philadelphia Warriors during the 1961-62 season."

"What about rebounds?"

Brady caught himself gaping and shut his mouth as he listened to her spiel off more statistics to Dortmeyer, a sports columnist for a Chicago newspaper.

"He had two thousand fifty-two rebounds that year."

Dortmeyer looked impressed.

Brady was, too. "I thought you didn't know anything about sports," he said quietly when she'd finished her conversation with the men.

"I've been reading biographies, sports newspapers and magazines."

"Reading?"

Smiling, she looked pleased with herself. ''To learn the games.''

Why? For him? Even Kirsten had never bothered to take an interest in what was important to him. Why would Maggie do that if she didn't care?

Silently he swore. It was dumb to make so much of something so simple. This couldn't go beyond what they had now. No matter what he was beginning to feel for her, he wouldn't let it.

Chapter Seven

Four hectic days passed. Maggie awakened before dawn to the sound of thunder. For the past week, clouds had hung in the sky, threatening a downpour, but not a drop had fallen. Until this morning. She listened to the heavy pounding of it, falling with hearty decisiveness.

She rolled over in bed and buried her head beneath her pillow. She had hours before she had to get up, slip on the lacy dress that she would wear only once and go to the chapel. Sleep would make the time pass quickly. Sleep would keep her from thinking too much about what she was going to do today.

During the past week, she'd managed to act overjoyed when an excited Deidre and a few other friends had thrown a surprise bridal shower for her. Attentively, she'd listened to the minister's instructions at the rehearsal last night. Afterward, she'd smiled at appropriate times during the rehearsal dinner. Brady had squeezed her hand encouragingly a few times. Her brother had sent her a supportive grin. The small dinner with friends and family, including Brady's parents, had been the most difficult moment. The deception to people who cared about them plagued her with guilt, and she wondered how many more moments could be this emotionally demanding.

Today might be even harder. Closing her eyes, she strived to go back to sleep. This would be the last time she would sleep alone for a while. A husband would be beside her in bed. He would be a part of her life for months.

Listening to the ticking of the clock, she remembered that they had to do whatever was necessary to succeed. The house, once so important to her, no longer dominated her motivations. One little tow-headed boy with a quick grin and beautiful blue eyes needed her to help his daddy. His welfare made the duplicity easier to accept.

With that thought, she went back to sleep. When she awoke hours later, she hustled to take a shower. Instead of the traditional bridal gown, she had traipsed to several small, exclusive boutiques and chosen a tea-length dress, a Victorian-style gown with a high neck and laced bodice.

Showered, and in her panties and bra, she slipped on a knee-length silk kimono and wandered toward the window and stared at a heavy pewter sky. A noon rain still pounded at the pavement. Hardly an auspicious start. Three-hundred-plus days a year the sun shone in Phoenix. Today, on her wedding day, it had to rain. Where were the singing birds, the shining sun, the scent of orange blossoms that usually symbolized marriage?

Maggie teetered on a myriad of emotions. Anxiousness led the list as she thought overlong about the day ahead. She had to calm down before Deidre arrived, glowing and more excited than she was. Count to ten. She did four times before she settled the nerves urging her to call up her brother and tell him she'd changed her mind.

She gave herself a few quick reminders. The marriage would be temporary. She wasn't committing to Brady for life. This was not a match meant to last forever.

By the time Deidre arrived, looking pretty in a brilliant blue dress with a scooped neck, Maggie had applied makeup. She'd taken more time than usual with it, and excused such behavior to playing her part and trying to look like a woman who wanted to be beautiful and please her new husband.

"You don't look nervous at all."

"There's no reason to be, is there?"

"Of course not." Deidre stared at her reflection in the mirror. "You're marrying the man you love."

Maggie finished attaching pearls to her ears and considered how to distract her friend. "Your bouquet is in the refrigerator."

Deidre swept from the room. Maggie heard her squeal of delight. "Yours is beautiful, Maggie."

She'd thought so, too, when she'd seen the nosegay of pale pink rosebuds and white camellias with baby's breath that Brady had had delivered.

"You look beautiful."

Maggie had never thought of herself that way, but she did feel prettier today than she ever had.

"Do you have everything?"

Maggie met her stare in the mirror. "What's everything?"

"Something borrowed?"

"These used to be my grandmother's earrings," Maggie returned, pointing to one dangling at her earlobe.

"Something new?"

"This," Maggie said, holding out her arms to show off the dress she'd just slipped on.

"Something old?" Deidre asked while zipping it for her.

"My shoes."

"And something blue."

"Nothing blue." Maggie couldn't help smiling.

With her announcement that she was wearing nothing blue, Deidre scowled at her in the mirror. "You have to have something blue."

"Don't panic." Maggie pointed at the slim blue ribbon in the bouquet.

Deidre heaved a sigh of relief. "Thank goodness."

"Now, can we leave?" Maggie asked, wanting as little time alone with her friend as possible. She only relaxed when she was with Brady. With everyone else, she fretted that they would ask too many questions about this whirlwind romance and hastily arranged marriage.

"I'm so, so happy for you." Deidre hugged her tightly.

Maggie saw the tears of joy in her friend's eyes and felt shame about the deceit rise within her. Unable to tell the truth, she simply took Deidre's hands in hers. "I can hardly wait until your wedding day."

Deidre blinked watery eyes and gave a little laugh. "I may have to hog-tie Henry before that will happen," she answered lightly. Seriousness slipped over her face immediately. "But what woman wants to marry a man if he doesn't love her?"

Maggie disagreed. This was the only way, the safest way to marry. No emotional involvement meant no hard feelings when it was over.

They drew away from each other with the ring of the doorbell. Punctual as always, her brother had arrived to drive them to the chapel. And she had just reached a point of no return, Maggie knew.

With her arm hooked in Bennett's, Maggie grabbed a long breath when she stood later at the end of the aisle as the organist began playing the wedding march.

"I haven't told you yet," Bennett said softly. "But you look beautiful."

She felt different in the dress. No wonder most women yearned for this moment. It was sort of like a fairy tale. "I hope you know what we're doing here."

A thread of concern crept into his voice. "Want to back out now?"

Anticipation hummed through her. "No, I'm ready." Nerves dancing in her stomach, she took the first step toward Brady standing at the altar.

Wearing a black tux, Brady listened to the first familiar chords and pushed aside a jab of uneasiness as he spotted Maggie with Bennett coming closer. Until that moment, he'd been tied in knots with worry that she would have second thoughts and jilt him at the altar.

His doubts abated, he flashed a brief smile at his sister seated beside his parents in the first pew. They returned smiles, their lips curving while their eyes carried questions. When he'd greeted them at the airport, they'd indicated their surprise about the rushed marriage. No one had asked the inevitable question regarding an unexpected pregnancy. After the wedding, after they'd returned to Florida, when he was sure they wouldn't slip up and tell someone that the marriage was one of convenience, he planned to explain everything.

He pushed aside anxiousness resulting from his dishonesty to people who mattered so much to him. For a while, he had to play the enamored groom. That wasn't hard to do at all, he acknowledged as Maggie grew closer. Not hard at all. She looked lovely. Romantic in the lacy dress.

Traditional vows were recited. He remembered saying them. Remembered slipping the gold band on her finger that connected with the engagement ring. But he never took his eyes off of her. And he decided "lovely" was too mild a description. She looked stunning.

Maggie didn't relax until she and Brady were in the car and on the way to the hotel her brother had booked for the reception. Instead of a small reception at his apartment, he'd insisted that the hotel was more serviceable to accommodate all the guests. Maggie could hardly argue with his practical decision. That didn't mean nerves weren't jumping within her. "Do

you think everyone is believing this?'' she whispered
to Brady during a quiet moment alone before they
entered the hotel to greet their wedding guests.

"Even I'm having a hard time not believing it,''
he teased. Tempted by the lace that was high at her
throat, he let his fingers skim across the edge of the
feminine fabric.

Maggie stilled. Why did pleasure slither through
her with even his simplest touch? Doing her best to
keep her edginess at bay as the wedding night loomed
closer, she teased, "Are we practicing again?''

Truthfully, Brady was having a hard time separat-
ing what was real and pretense between them. "We'd
better go in, Mrs. McQueen.''

The sound of what was now her own name overwhelmed her.

She was legally his wife. It seemed odd. From the
time she'd entered adolescence, endured her parents'
tug-of-war over her, she'd never planned to be a wife.
Yet she'd willingly entered into this marriage.

The touch of his hand enveloping hers brought her
mind back to the moment. Smiles in place, she and
Brady entered the room filled with their guests.

Her brother had done well. The champagne was
chilled. Flowers scented the air. Sparkling chandeliers
reflected the multitude of colors of women dressed in
finery. A three-piece band played music meant for
dancing.

His parents greeted them first. "We're sorry we
didn't get a chance to meet your mother, Maggie.''

Maggie fought to hold on to a smile. "Maybe some
other time.''

Brady kept a hand firm on Maggie's waist. Two

days ago, he'd asked if her mother was coming to the wedding. He'd been stunned when she'd said that she'd sent the invitation and had never received the RSVP.

"I haven't seen my mother in the past seven years" had been her explanation. "She used to call once in a while around my birthday, but her life is busy. I think she's on husband number four."

End of subject, Brady mused.

"We're still in shock," Brady's dad was saying with a glance at his wife, who stood beside him.

Maggie kept smiling to hide her nervousness. Brady's dad was tall and lean, and had sharper features than his son, but the hair color and the blue eyes were so like Brady's that when his father smiled at her she saw both Brady and Conor. Close beside her, Brady squeezed her hand a second before his mother opened her arms to hug her.

"But thrilled," his mother said, beaming.

Not completely, Maggie thought as she saw the flicker of worry in his mother's eyes. Trim, a few inches shorter than Maggie, blond and tanned, Brady's mother had been warm and welcoming ever since they'd met. She was a woman who hugged easily, touched freely. She had sparkling pale blue eyes, perceptive ones. This woman could read her son's expression too well. She wasn't fooled. She could tell that he didn't look at his new wife with love in his eyes.

Maggie nudged a smile forward, then sort of swayed toward Brady like a new bride needing her husband's closeness.

Everyone grinned.

Brady tightened his hold on her waist. There was no way to prevent parental annoyance with him. His mother would be upset when she learned the truth. He noted that the smile she was wearing was growing thin. She wanted an explanation. He expected she wouldn't be pleased with him, or his dishonesty, when the marriage didn't last forever. Hell, when it came to an end in a few months from now.

To his relief, everyone's attention shifted to Bennett with his request that guests raise their fluted champagne glasses in a toast to the happy couple. In response, Brady did the expected. He lowered his head and kissed Maggie. Cheers filled the room.

It was all so dreamlike. Maggie felt as if she were standing outside herself and watching everything.

The evening wore on, people congratulating them, kissing their cheeks. They danced and nibbled from the array of food on the buffet table. They posed for the photographer and cut the three-tiered cake.

And through every minute, Brady remained tight at her side and played the adoring new husband. Maggie knew it was foolish, but she felt special, treasured. Or maybe her headiness was a result of drinking too much champagne, she reasoned. "I've had my fill of this."

Brady noted the unmistakable sparkle of intoxication in her eyes before she turned away to set the half-finished glass on the tray of a white-jacketed employee passing by. "You don't want more?"

"If I'm not careful," she said on a soft laugh, "you'll have to carry me out of here."

"It would be my pleasure."

Unprepared for such words, Maggie met his eyes.

She shouldn't be ridiculous, but she felt a little thrill, nonetheless. No man had ever offered to carry her anywhere.

"You two are doing a great job," Bennett said, suddenly sidling close to them. "I guess now that the evening's almost over, I'll give you my wedding present."

"Bennett, don't be silly. Why would you give us one? It's bad enough all these other people did." Maggie had already decided all gifts would be returned immediately following her and Brady's breakup.

"This one is more for Brady than both of you," he said with a teasing grin, and turned away, only to appear seconds later with Conor in his arms.

Joy whipped through Brady with such quickness he thought his knees might buckle.

"I learned late yesterday that your petition for temporary custody went through," Bennett said while transferring Conor to his father's arms.

"Da." Conor flung his arms around Brady's neck.

"What did Olivia say?" Brady asked, holding his son tightly to him.

Bennett grinned. "Nothing. She glared."

Concern rose within Maggie. "Aren't you surprised she didn't say anything?"

"She wasn't ready for a showdown," Brady responded. He sounded calm, but deep down, he was scared. Hell, he was terrified for his son. Never would he want to see him as confused and insecure as Kirsten had been.

"She'll make more trouble for you," Bennett declared. "But for now, you keep him until the court date."

Elation overwhelmed Brady, tightening his chest with the pressure of the emotion. "I don't have to take Conor back to her?"

Bennett shook his head. "Nope. You keep him."

A great weight seemed to have been lifted from him. On a laugh, he swung toward Maggie and kissed her hard.

Maggie felt happiness for him. She also viewed the moment as a reminder. Conor's presence emphasized why they were really here, why she was wearing a wedding ring. "We could leave now," she said, certain Brady was anxious to go home with his son.

"You wouldn't mind leaving?"

Actually, she felt drained from all the pretense. "Whenever you're ready."

Despite her agreement and his urgency, it still took what seemed like hours to get away from guests and say goodbye to his parents, who planned a flight home at midnight.

With a sleeping Conor in the back seat of Brady's car, they drove toward home. To avert his mind from the custody hearing still to be faced, Brady guided their conversation away from his problem and concentrated on hers. "Why didn't you invite your cousin?" he asked while negotiating the car onto the final road toward his house.

"She knew what was happening." Maggie ended her viewing of passing scenery. "And we're not friendly. It didn't make sense for me to invite her if she wouldn't be happy for me."

Brady braked on the driveway and switched off the

ignition before shifting toward her and draping an arm over the steering wheel.

"If I had invited her, she would have believed that I only did it so she could confirm that I got married," she said, clarifying her previous comment.

He couldn't help grinning. "Maggie, you're beginning to get the hang of this idea."

But she wasn't, not really. The wedding had taken place. Now what? she wondered.

Brady carried a sleeping Conor to his room, slipped off his shoes and pants, and changed his diaper. His son never stirred. With Conor dressed in his Winnie the Pooh pajamas, Brady sat for a few minutes in the rocker Kirsten had insisted on having in the nursery, and he held his son.

He wanted to cuddle him tightly but didn't dare. If he held him as close and snugly as he wanted to, he could hurt him. So he resigned himself to staring at his son's bow-shaped mouth, to listening to his steady, even breaths, and took comfort in Conor's peacefulness.

"You're home now," he whispered. Pressing his lips to Conor's forehead, he eased him down to the mattress, then placed a blanket on him. "I promise. I'm never letting you go again."

Maggie stood alone in the bedroom with only a carryall bag containing her possessions. She assumed tomorrow she would have to bring her things over. Tired, she yawned. Before this, with so much to do for the wedding, she hadn't allowed herself to contemplate overlong the wedding night.

Nervous, she spent a long time in the bathroom.

She washed and creamed her face and brushed her teeth before wandering into the bedroom. At the sight of Brady, she jumped.

Standing before the closet, he looked over his shoulder at her. "Is the room all right?"

Maggie clutched her robe and nodded. Actually, she liked the masculine room with its rich, dark furniture.

"Kirsten had liked everything white."

He was telling her this was his room, not his and Kirsten's. "When I was a child, I had an all-white bedroom, my mother's choice. I always felt as if I shouldn't mess anything."

A breakthrough, Brady realized. That was the first time she'd freely mentioned her childhood to him. Curiosity piqued, he stood still a moment longer. But more than questions about her past kept him there. Her shining hair hung loose to her shoulders. With that trace of shyness he found endearing, she avoided his stare. "Would you like a cup of coffee? It's made."

Maggie jumped at a chance to get out of the bedroom. She knew the marriage bargain included them sleeping together for one night so she wouldn't have to lie about their relationship in court, but she wasn't ready. "I'd love a cup."

Brady grabbed his terry-cloth robe and headed for the door.

"I'll meet you in the kitchen."

By the time Maggie got there, he'd poured coffee for both of them.

Sensing she would run before being backed into a corner, he asked what he thought she would consider inconsequential conversation. "What was your grandfather like?"

"He was wonderful," she said with deep affection as she settled on an adjacent chair at the table. A smile lit her face with a remembrance. "And eccentric. He always sat in the front seat with the chauffeur." She would have been lost without him.

He could tell she'd loved the old coot who had caused her this problem, but what about her parents? "You didn't live with your parents?"

"They were divorced." Maggie stared at the dark brew in her cup.

"Divorce is hard on kids," he said, guessing she viewed her grandfather as her rock during a disturbing time in her life.

"And custody battles are devastating to a child," Maggie said simply.

Fate had stepped in, he realized. Only someone who'd gone through the misery of a custody battle would have understood what he'd been trying to protect Conor from. When she looked away, he pressed harder. "How old were you when it happened?"

Her blue eyes darkened as he revived memories she'd long buried. "Eight," she answered. *And what she'd felt hadn't mattered.* "You should know these kind of court cases can go on forever. If you don't get this settled, Conor might be touched by it."

"How long were your parents in court in the custody fight?"

"Off and on for three years." For his son, to protect that sweet little boy from what she'd endured, she would do anything. "Custody battles are so ugly, Brady, so full of anger."

"Your parents must have loved you very much to fight that long for you."

Neither of them had.

With her silence, Brady made himself prod, aware she would clam up again if he let her. "What aren't you saying?"

Maggie gave up trying to fool him. Somehow he knew what to say to penetrate the wall that usually halted people from probing too deeply. "They were used to fighting. I was simply something else for them to fight about. Each of them had their own interests."

"You had a lousy childhood," he declared.

"It wasn't wonderful," Maggie admitted. "My father lived for his work. My mother preferred a more carnal satisfaction. She made the gossipers happy as they followed her escapades with the many men in her life. She still can't live without one."

But *she* could. She'd made damn sure of that, Brady realized. "Who got custody of you when the battle was over?"

"They both did. The judge decided I should live six months with each of them."

"Was that difficult?"

She released a soft, mirthless laugh. "It was almost as bad as listening to them tear each other apart."

As she gave him a weary look, he hunched forward to take her hand. He didn't want her to close up on him now. "Why? Because you were bounced around from one place to the other?"

"Because I learned the truth then." Her back straightened as if preparing for a jolt. "They only wanted me when they couldn't have me." She'd never said those words to anyone except Bennett.

Brady tilted his head. Were those the words of a woman who still saw memories with a child's eyes? "You might have believed that. Kids don't always see things the way—"

"Brady, I didn't misinterpret anything. They didn't want me. Whoever had me shipped me off to school. You see, they fought to have me." She gave him a sad smile. "But they didn't want me. Each of them merely wanted to be the winner. They wanted to hurt each other. It was all a power play. When my father won the final custody suit because he had more money and power, my mother disappeared from my life."

Maggie released a weary sigh. Even discussing that time exhausted her. "Until I lived with my grandfather, I had never spent a holiday away from school. Both my parents would call, say they were sorry but something had come up. They couldn't come and get me. Of course, the check, my Christmas present, was in the mail."

Self-absorbed, selfish people. They didn't know what love was. Not even love for their child. He wanted to swear. He wanted to gather her close.

Maggie had purged herself of tears years ago. Tears didn't change the disappointment, the emptiness she'd felt.

Lightly, he caressed a strand of her hair. It was clear now why she believed that she didn't need anyone. He stared at her with admiration, wondering how she had become such a reasonable, normal person when she'd come from such dysfunctional people. "Where was Bennett during all of this?"

She stared blankly at him for a moment. "Being

older, he went through a year of the bouncing back and forth, then left to attend Oxford.''

And had been less affected by the lack of parental love. ''Did he know how bad it was for you?''

''He knew what it had been like, but when he called me, I never told him how miserable I was.''

''Why didn't you tell Bennett?'' He knew his friend's love for his sister.

''I didn't want him worrying.''

Brady sipped his coffee and eyed her over the rim of the cup. How much could he ask and not upset her? ''What about your grandfather?''

Maggie pressed the cold cup to her warm cheek. An image of John Michael Buchanan, a sweet, gentle, giant of a man with a head of white hair and a bushy white mustache, came forward in her mind.

''Where was he? Did he ever realize that you'd been...?'' Damn. What was he going to say? Ignored? He couldn't finish the question that might slice through her.

Maggie quickly came to her grandfather's defense. ''My mother was on her fourth husband when my father died. She didn't come home from Spain for the funeral.''

Her mother had to have known her daughter needed her. What kind of woman would turn her back on her child at a time like that? Brady couldn't imagine not being near for Conor if he was hurt, emotionally or physically.

''That's when my grandfather took over. He held me at the funeral. The moment we got home, he called my mother, told her that she'd had her chance, and he was petitioning the court for custody of me.''

Hearing the unhappiness she'd endured, Brady vowed that Conor would never experience anything like that. If he'd had doubts before about this marriage, they'd left as she'd told him about the sadness in her childhood. This marriage was a must to protect his son.

"Everything was better then."

How simple she made that sound. He hated the practiced smile she presented to him. He knew now why she hadn't expected her mother at their wedding. "What is it that's in here?" Hunching forward, gently Brady placed a fingertip to her chest in a totally unsensual way.

He had no idea how much more she'd told him about her thoughts and feelings than she'd ever shared with other people. "I heard two people who once were in love verbally attacking each other. How can people claim to love another and the next moment want to destroy each other?" Time had healed the wounds, but she would never forget.

He started to reach forward to touch her hand but stopped himself, and fought a longing to comfort her. "You aren't like those two people, Maggie. Just because they didn't know how to love, doesn't mean you don't."

"You might be right." Her chin lifted. "I am different from them. I've seen the pain that love caused. I don't want any part of it."

Brady drained the coffee in his cup. He couldn't argue with her. In the name of love, he'd known his share of heartache. "It's been a long day."

Maggie didn't move. "Yes," she answered as best she could. Her mouth felt dry, her throat thick.

Brady made himself stand. "I'm going to bed." He moved to the doorway and stilled. "Maggie, if you're staying up, you'll have to turn out the light." He wanted her a lot more than he'd realized, he knew at that moment. "Sleep well."

That brought her head up. "Where are you going?"

"To sleep in the guest bedroom."

Kind, he was kinder than she'd expected.

Chapter Eight

During the next two weeks, they acted like the blissful couple. Maggie collected bare essentials from her apartment, but soon needed to make decisions about the rest of her possessions.

Through breakfast this morning, Conor had poked unenthusiastically at the bacon and scrambled eggs his father had prepared. For appearances' sake, Brady had insisted they closet themselves away from everyone. Newlyweds, he reminded Maggie, liked time to themselves. So he'd taken vacation time from the newspaper. During those days, Brady had been companionable, humorous and extremely careful not to touch her. Maggie believed that was best. Nothing lasted forever, not potent and passionate emotions or the promises people made because of them.

"So you're all right about staying alone with

Conor?'' Brady asked not for the first time since they'd finished breakfast.

Showered, shaved and dressed to leave, he acted hesitant about going out the door. ''It's no problem,'' Maggie insisted with only a glance at him. When she didn't look at him, she thought more clearly. With his regular housekeeper still visiting a relative in Albuquerque, he'd suggested earlier that he call a babysitter. Maggie had reached deep inside herself for courage of a different sort, and had protested when he'd gone to make the phone call. The idea was ridiculous. People would wonder why she, if she loved him and if she wanted to be a real mother to Conor, wasn't taking care of Conor.

Brady had agreed that she made good sense.

Maggie wished now that she hadn't. She really had no idea how to care for Conor. Since their marriage, Brady had taken full responsibility for his son.

''You have my phone number to page me. Right?''

''Right.''

Brady checked the clock above the stove. This evening's home basketball game meant getting a few interviews this morning from the home team and the visitors, three-time world champions. ''If you need me—''

''We'll be fine,'' she said with forced gaiety.

''See you.'' He wanted to kiss her goodbye. He wanted to hold her, tell her how much he enjoyed something as simple as watching a sitcom on television and laughing with her at the actors' antics. He wanted too much because he was too aware of her. He knew better than to start believing in this make-believe marriage, but he'd liked being married. He enjoyed having a woman near. No, he liked having this woman near. He'd begun to look forward to the late-night talks with Maggie. He looked for the smile that sprang to her face when Conor did something comical. He anticipated her subtle fragrance before she entered a room. Mostly, he'd begun to yearn for the touch of her hand on him when she wasn't thinking about what she was doing. And all of that was wrong.

"You'll be back before dinner, won't you?"

Brady bent forward to kiss Conor. "Before dinner." He noticed her quick, unsteady smile. It had looked so tentative that while driving away he was tempted several times to make a U-turn and go back home.

Why had she volunteered if she was nervous? Fighting morning rush hour traffic to the business center of the city, he tapped his fingers impatiently on the steering wheel. He knew she had no experience. Women like her and Kirsten learned the fine art of entertaining via butlers and maids. Any experience they had with children included the presence of nannies. He remembered how much he and Kirsten had fought regarding one. He'd refused to hire one. With her mother prompting her, she'd been adamant about needing one. Brady had compromised and agreed to ask Renie if she'd take on the job. After she'd agreed, for nearly three months, Renie had been scrutinized before Kirsten and, he assumed, her mother had given her their approval.

Brady switched lanes as he neared the hotel where the visiting basketball team was booked and zipped into the parking garage. It was dumb to be concerned about Conor being with someone as responsible as Maggie.

No, it wasn't, he argued with himself. He knew the trials and tribulations of spending an afternoon with someone on the verge of being two years old.

Would Maggie feel overwhelmed? What if she hated it? All her life other people had taken care of her, waited on *her*. She'd probably never faced sticky hands or spilled milk before.

Dammit, he should have called a regular baby-sitter. He shouldn't have left them alone. What if he came home and she announced that she was halting their agreement? He might think his son was wonderful, but someone else, especially someone who'd been pampered and lived an almost antiseptic existence, might view him as a messy rug rat.

Maggie liked kids; she really did. But she'd never spent time alone with one.

Briefly, Conor watched two talking dinosaurs on the television and swayed with the music that accompanied a flying whale's trip over a locked gate to free himself and his friends, who included a crab and several penguins.

Beginning to think this might be easier than she expected, Maggie settled on the sofa and tucked her legs beneath her. She opened the book in her hands, but never read a word.

His interest in the television show waning, Conor toddled toward her. "Cakes."

Maggie set the book down in her lap. "No, I don't think your father would want you to have cake."

"Outside," he asked while pointing at the door.

She smiled with relief that he'd accepted her no without a protest. "That would be okay."

Conor was already at the door. "Cake."

Don't get too smug, she realized. She'd noticed that Brady had practiced a lot of patience to outsmart the two-year-old. "No, you can't have cake," she repeated firmly as she recalled reading somewhere that a parent must be consistent. "But you can go outside." She opened the back door for him and followed him onto a portion of the patio at the side of the house that was fenced off from the backyard pool. Maggie watched him head for a green turtle-shaped sandbox. Oh, why did she agree to this? She had no idea how to deal with children. She'd had few friends as a child. She'd never even been around friends' children.

"Off."

Maggie had already started to lift the turtle's lid. This might not be too difficult. At least they were communicating without Brady as an interpreter, she thought with some encouragement and settled on the closest lawn chair. While Conor played in his sandbox, she would read a book that she'd bought yesterday when they'd gone out for a family outing at the shopping mall.

"Cake." Standing in the middle of the sandbox, Conor held a small green cup out to her.

Realization hit her finally.

"You do," Conor insisted.

Maggie pushed to a stand. "I can do this," she murmured to herself, and dropped to a squat outside the sandbox. Guessing what he wanted, she reached into the sandbox for one of the wooden spoons. It felt gritty beneath her fingers. The few times she'd gone to the beach, she'd hated the texture of sand beneath her feet.

"Me do." Conor dug with another spoon and dumped only half of the sand into the cup.

Maggie dumped the filled cup over onto a board she'd guessed was meant for holding his sand creations, especially his cakes of sand.

"Cake," Conor said again. His body swayed first left, then right. "Appy. Appy."

Maggie smiled. "Happy birthday?"

A knock-your-socks-off grin so like his father's sprang to his face, and he swayed some more while he sang his rendition of the song.

Pleased with herself, Maggie created several more sand cakes with him, and she never returned to the book she'd brought outside.

Instead, she kicked a toy football to him, took turns with him at smacking at a plastic golf ball, and while he rode his fire engine, she made a discovery. She *really did* like children. There was something magical about Conor's smiles that swept warmth through her.

"Down," Conor said, grabbing her attention and tugging her hand.

Maggie looked back toward a cushioned patio chair, but Conor tugged again and plopped down on the hard cement.

Maggie followed suit, tucking her legs beneath her.

"Car." He handed one to her.

This will get easier, she promised herself. But in the meantime, his every request puzzled her. Staring at the car, she wondered what she was supposed to do with it.

Conor pushed it around on the cement. "Zoom. Zoom."

Maggie copied his actions. "Zoom. Zoom," she said, moving the car beside his.

It seemed like such a simple thing to do, but Conor rewarded her with a smile that brightened his whole face, which made her feel as if she were the smartest, most wonderful person he knew. With Conor's giggle, she laughed and wrapped her arms around him.

He hugged her back hard. "Aggie."

"You are so wonderful," Maggie murmured, touching the silky texture of his hair. She loved the feel of the small boy snuggled against her. There's danger here, she warned herself, but didn't—couldn't—release Conor from her embrace.

That was how Brady found them. Weary after shoving his way through a crowd of fans and past security guards to get an interview, he dragged himself from the car later that afternoon. His tiredness disappeared with the sight of them sitting close, Maggie's dark head and his son's fair one close together. After Kirsten had died, he'd always assumed he would go through life alone. He still believed that, but seeing them together looked right. As he took a step closer, Maggie looked up. "It went all right?" he asked, wishing she would smile.

"Fine." Better than she'd imagined. "Are you home for a while now?"

"Sure." Since she didn't look frazzled and Conor wasn't wailing, he relaxed. "Why?"

"I need to meet the contractor at my grandfather's house."

Married now, she saw no reason why she couldn't

begin renovation plans on the house. She'd picked up several wallpaper books that contained reproduction designs from the eighteenth and nineteenth centuries. She'd located someone to relead the antique stained-glass windows. And yesterday she'd called a contractor about beginning structural repairs.

"Want company?"

Maggie doubted he'd find the renovation interesting. "You don't have to go along."

"I'd like to." He'd spent the day away and had missed both of them. "Do you mind that I want to spend time with you?"

How odd, she mused. They were married, yet she felt as if they'd just met. "I like being with you, too."

Progress, Brady mused. "I'll get Conor's car seat."

Maggie felt an idiotic grin on her face. It widened when she saw Conor's frown over the sand sprinkled on the toe of his sneaker.

Little fingers brushed some of it away, then he raised his head to Maggie. "Yucky."

She laughed and bent down to help him brush the sand off.

It was then she caught a whiff of an undeniable odor. "Somehow, I think your daddy knew what he was doing when he suggested he get the car seat."

"Bye?"

Maggie kissed the tip of his nose. "Yes, we're going bye," she answered, realizing that the words *car seat* had triggered that response from Conor. Lifting him in her arms, she nuzzled his neck. "But first you need your diaper changed."

She never expected that to be difficult. She'd

watched Brady change Conor's diapers often enough, so she was confident she could.

Minutes later, she balled one diaper in frustration and snatched up a second, finally aware the tape went from the back to the front. Good-natured, Conor simply smiled up at her as if cognizant that one of them needed a wealth of patience at the moment.

One step into her grandparents' sedate, refined home, and Brady scooped Conor into his arms. Though the house needed repairs, the living room still contained too many expensive antiques for his son's inquisitive fingers. Behind him, the contractor was giving Maggie his assessment.

"You need thicker rafters for the roof. They only used two-by-fours."

"But I don't want to change the authenticity of the house."

"Telling you like it is," he said, with a glance at Brady.

"Show me," Maggie insisted.

"You want to climb up to the attic with me?"

"That or tell me exactly what the problem is."

Brady looked away to veil a grin. Beneath the lamb's gentleness, a lion lurked.

"Roof is sagging, ma'am. There's six layers of roofing up there. Come out front with me. I'll show you what I mean."

"I'm having the roof done. Can you use the original materials, then?" Maggie glanced back at Brady standing in the hallway and holding Conor. She'd noticed that he hadn't set him down since they'd entered the house. "I need to talk to him for a minute."

"I'll take Conor outside."

She nodded, but her attention was already sliding back to the contractor.

Every day with her revealed something new to him about her, Brady reflected. With Conor in his arms, he stepped onto the terrace. Maggie had retained a quaintness outside to match the house. A border of flowers, bright with a riot of color, circled the gazebo. A flower garden of soft yellow flowers, along with dozens of others, the colors playing off one another, filled a patch of ground to the right of the cobble-stoned terrace.

"It's pretty, isn't it?" Maggie said as she joined him at the edge of the terrace.

"Nice," he said honestly. "Really nice."

She thought his compliment genuine. "When my grandmother was alive, she would plant a different color every season." Like her, Maggie took great pride in the flowers. "She would plan it so colors blended at every level, like tulips in the back and shorter violas and poppies in front."

"This takes a lot of work, doesn't it?"

"I enjoy it," Maggie answered easily. "The ones that look like dandelions are *Pseudonarcissus pumilus plenus*." She caught his puzzled frown. "Rip van Winkles. They're really miniature daffodils. Over there," she said, pointing to the edge of the terrace, "is a wildflower mix."

"Ma'am?" The contractor hung back, lingering at the doorway. "Here's the estimate you asked for."

"I'll be right back."

As Maggie whirled away, Conor squirmed in Brady's arms. "Down," he insisted.

Unsure how much longer Maggie would be, Brady set a wiggly Conor down. A bird had already caught his eye. Arms outstretched, he rushed toward it to catch it.

Brady smiled and looked back to hear Maggie challenging the cost of ripping out old plaster.

"You're a tough lady to deal with," the man said, but Brady heard the note of admiration in the man's voice. "So are we agreeable to this?" he asked after scribbling a price.

Maggie gave him a smile guaranteed to curl his toes. "You'll start Monday?"

"See you Monday." He turned away, whistling.

"Was the news worse than you expected about the renovation?" Brady asked as she ambled toward him again.

"It has to be rewired and replumbed. I was told the other day that the fireplace would have to be re-bricked."

Brady said the obvious. "Lots of work."

"It usually costs more to renovate than build a house from scratch."

"Is it worth it?"

She sent him a smile, a dynamite smile. "It's always worthwhile to hold on to something valuable, no matter how much work it takes. That kind of thinking is a must if you belong to the Historical Preservation Society. We believe that work makes something even more valuable."

Brady didn't wonder how she could think that way and be so resistant to personal relationships. During the time since they'd met, he'd begun to understand her better. Sensitive, she showed a passion for something intangible, like the house. There was no risk. But in her personal life, she withdrew for one reason—to protect herself. "If you're ready to leave, I'll get Conor. We can stop for something to eat before I have to leave for the game." He would have preferred to go home, forget the game. The coolness of sunset had grayed the sky, and Conor's bedtime was near. Time with his son and her was all he cared about lately. "I never asked. Do you like Chinese food?"

"Love it."

Grinning, Brady swung away to call his son.

Conor shot from around behind a bush, his small hand gripping a bunch of flowers.

Brady frowned, aware of the time Maggie had spent nurturing the flowers in her garden. "Maggie, I'm sorry, he—"

She shook her head to silence him and squatted before Conor. "Are those for me?"

"Ya," he answered, a sunshiny smile sparkling in his eyes.

"Thank you, Conor."

"Elcome"

Maggie held the yanked blossoms and watched him toddle toward the birdbath.

"I am sorry," Brady said, regarding the blossoms pulled from the ground and left with such short stems that she couldn't even place them in a vase.

Maggie stared down at the broken stems of the orange zinnias and pinkish red petunias. She would place some in a vase. The others could float in water. "Flowers grow back," she said with a smile up at him. "It was a sweet thing for him to do."

Thank you, Maggie. Gratefulness for her understanding and sensitivity rushed through him. He stored the sight of them to memory, their heads bent, staring at the short-stemmed flowers, his son beaming over his gift to her, her smile filled with—what? Love? Love for his child? Yes, it had been love. And for as long as he lived, Brady would never forget the looks on their faces. Never.

Though Brady wasn't home, Maggie went through the nightly ritual that Conor seemed to love. She bathed him and gave him time to play with his favorite tub toy—a Sesame Street boat—then dressed him in his pajamas and supervised teeth-brushing time. His eyes were heavy when she was reading a book to him.

Sitting in the rocker, with Brady's son in her arms, she couldn't help thinking about him. Often their eyes met and held for long moments, yet he hadn't pushed her to complete her part of the marriage bargain. Maggie believed he was attracted to her, and whenever she thought about them together, she felt a little hitch in the vicinity of her heart. Another woman who believed in family and commitment and the forever kind of love that romantic books and songs proclaimed might fall under the spell of domesticity being weaved around them. She wouldn't.

She stood up to settle Conor in his bed. Despite previous thoughts, she admitted that there was something unbelievably fulfilling about doing this simple act.

By the time she finished making herself a cup of tea and had slipped on her nightgown and robe, the late news was on television. She settled in a chair to watch it and wait for Brady to return home.

Half an hour later she heard his car pulling onto the driveway. What seemed like several more minutes passed before he came through the door—frowning. "They won, didn't they?" she asked, because she couldn't fathom what had changed his mood since he left.

He nodded and shrugged out of his white windbreaker. He didn't drop to his favorite chair to watch the late news as he'd done the other times when he'd returned from covering a game. Instead, he walked to the window as if something was weighing heavily on his mind.

Maybe his mood hadn't changed, Maggie reflected. Nerves fluttered her stomach. Before he'd left for the game, he'd gotten a phone call. He'd seemed distracted after it. He'd forced smiles and had laughed less at his son's antics. She'd thought they'd had a good time at dinner. Maybe she didn't understand him as well as she thought. "Is there a problem?"

"A big one, I guess." Admitting to cowardliness irritated Brady, but he'd been gutless or he would have told her earlier what needed to be said. "Renie's coming home."

The housekeeper. So the time had come. "She lives in, doesn't she?" With his nod, Maggie imagined questions would plague the woman if she became aware of their separate bedrooms. "I'll put clean sheets on the bed in the guest bedroom. You'd better move your things back into your bedroom," Maggie said with a casualness that took effort. Not looking at him, she pushed herself off the sofa.

Brady felt like hell. The last thing he'd wanted to do was force himself into that bedroom with her. "Maggie?"

She stilled at the doorway and made herself look back at him.

"I'm sorry."

Brady stalled from joining her. He sat in the kitchen with a cup of coffee until exhaustion slipped over him. When he'd mentioned before that they needed a real marriage, she'd been reluctant. And he would never take a reluctant woman to bed.

Standing by the sink, he rinsed his coffee cup. If he had to, he could always get up in the middle of the night and take a cold shower.

Quietly, he moved into the dark bedroom. Squinting, he was able to see only an outline of her curled up on her side near the edge of the bed. Sharing a bed with her might prove the most difficult part of this plan. Need sprang forth as he just contemplated her warm softness brushing against him during sleep. He didn't fool himself into believing that a promise to keep to his side of the bed was enough to make that fact. He'd been married before, shared a bed night after night with a woman. Bodies curled toward each other for warmth. A head abandoned a pillow for the cushion of a shoulder. A hand curved around the sharp point of a hip. Legs tangled.

He could deal with this. Quietly, he eased into bed and stared at her back. He would wait until she was ready. Not feeling restful, he punched at his pillow then closed his eyes. He'd been exhausted earlier. Now he felt charged with enough energy to run sev-

eral miles. Maybe he should do that. Get out of the
room, away from her. He cursed softly when she
shifted and wriggled her rump against his loins. Turning his back to her, he closed his eyes. Go to sleep.
Don't think about her.

The feminine smile was enticing, teasing. The
woman moved close then backed away, a woman
wearing something filmy and flowing. She appeared
again as if in a fog, near once more, her long black
hair curling around him. Reaching out, he felt velvet
beneath his fingertips.

Then he heard a feminine moan of pleasure. It took
only a moment. Hovering between sleep and wake-
fulness, Brady pulled himself far enough away from
the dreamy haze to know where he was, who was
beside him. Again, he glided a hand down the
smoothness that he recognized had been Maggie's
thigh, and with lazy pleasure, ran his fingers up it
again. And again, she sighed with the sound of
delight.

Lowering his head, Brady murmured her name before he kissed the side of her neck, before he slipped
his hand beneath the silky nightie draped over her leg.
He might have stopped then, but Maggie turned to
her back. And in a welcoming move, her arms curled
around his shoulders. As she drew him to her, he
knew he should stop, should make her conscious of
him.

But he felt so much acceptance in the lips beneath
his. Was she aware? he wondered. To think that much
took effort. He savored the taste of her, marveled over
the way she looked bathed in moonlight, her skin like

porcelain, her hair dark and flowing over the white pillow. His mouth deepened on hers.

Another moan was sufficient encouragement. He scooted down, pressing light kisses to her breast. Desire tugging at him, he slipped the thin strap of the gown down her shoulder, found her breast. He felt her hands in his hair as he circled first one nipple and then the other with his tongue. "Maggie," he murmured.

Maggie didn't want to answer and end the fantasy she'd been drifting under. Until this moment, she'd been able to keep her eyes closed. Cowardly or not, she just didn't want to see his eyes, especially see any disappointment in them. She wasn't curvy or full-breasted. She was slim, angular, with small breasts. She'd always thought her legs too long, even too thin. She knew she wasn't centerfold material, and he'd known so many other women. Kirsten had been a few inches shorter than her, fleshier with full, high breasts. That was his ideal woman, not someone like her.

She didn't want to remind him. He might stop. And there was too much to experience, too much to enjoy. She felt too much pleasure as she let her hands roam over his muscular back. Needs she had ignored, fantasies that she had never admitted to, desire that she had never allowed bombarded her, promising to shatter her senses.

No, she couldn't stop him. Not now with him slithering the nightgown down her hips. Naked, she squeezed her eyes tighter. What if he decided to stop now? Then she wouldn't be able to touch more of his taut skin.

Relief slithered through her. His mouth had returned to her, but not to her lips. He'd draped himself across her. Slowly, tauntingly, his lips traced a path over the curve of her breast, along her rib cage and across her belly. She thought she would go mad with the pleasure of it as her senses took over. She was aware of the hardness of her nipples, of the wetness between her thighs, of the hard probing part of him pushing at her hip. She was aware of his mouth, hot and firm; of his tongue, greedy with a hunger that stunned her, stroking across her thigh. Heat flooded her. Sensation tingled its way through her to her toes. Muscles tightened. The world exploded. She thought it the most wonderful feeling she'd ever had. And she wanted to beg him, the way a small child pleaded for candy, for more. More. Please, give me more.

Close to the edge, Brady groaned and buried his face in her neck. When she pushed her length against him, when her legs opened to make room for his, any thoughts of stopping abandoned him. He pressed his mouth against her ear, inhaled deeply the scent of her, wanting to keep it in his memory.

With an urgency he couldn't curb, he slipped into her. Briefly he felt resistance, not from her but from her body, and knew he was the first. Then he was fully in. Flesh, hot and damp, met flesh. There had been others since Kirsten. None had enveloped him so deeply. He felt as if he'd belonged nowhere else.

He'd been right, he knew now. Within her was an intensity, a passion, a heat that had been waiting. He was the first to find it, and he realized the gift being given. But that was the last coherent thought he had.

He drove deeper, each thrust harder, until his breaths were ragged, torn from his throat, until nothing mattered, nothing except her and the need to fill her, to hear her cry of pleasure.

Chapter Nine

Brady released a shuddery breath. He should have
been gentler. He should have guessed how innocent
she really was. "Are you okay?"

Okay? She felt dazed. Ecstatic. Embarrassed. He
knew now that she'd never slept with any man before.
She felt heat in her face. Was it from humiliation? Or
was she glowing? Or was that something made up in
books?

"Maggie, are you?" He wished she would answer,
prayed she didn't start crying. Had he hurt her? Was
that why she was so quiet? "Listen, Maggie, I—"
Her touch silenced him.

With her fingertips, Maggie lightly stroked the
short stubble of his beard along his jaw. "I wasn't
sure what to do."

In the moonlit room, her skin was bathed by a silvery sheen. She was lovelier than he'd ever seen her. "I couldn't have asked for anything different," he murmured against her collarbone.

Maggie ran a hand over the back of his head. He was just saying that, wasn't he? He was trying to make her feel good. There wouldn't be more times. That had been the obligatory night of sex to make their marriage legal, so she wouldn't have to lie in court about them having been together.

Then he spread kisses down her throat.

Brady heard her sigh. He'd thought of moving, giving her room to breathe, but he couldn't distance his mind or body from the warm softness of her body. Lightly, he skimmed the round curve of her hip, then drew back and peered in the darkness at her. A frown etched a faint line between her brows. "I know, no complications." He thought that's what she would want to hear, what he should say to her. "But I do want you, Maggie."

She sighed again. It was so difficult to think when he was touching her. "I want you, too."

Brady closed his eyes. He wanted to tell her that what she'd given him was valued, treasured, but he kept silent about how special she was to him. "We could be lovers," he whispered instead.

His breath warmed her breast. Eyes closed, she gathered him tighter to her as his mouth hovered close to her nipple. "We wouldn't have to lie in court about our marriage being a real one," she murmured, amazed she was thinking so clearly now when he was covering her breasts with kisses.

"Maggie?"

"Yes." She moaned in response to his hand heating her belly, then cupping her.

"I've never wanted anyone as much as I want you right now," he said, because he wanted her to know. This time he would be gentler, he'd give her something unforgettable. Even as desire hummed through him, he made himself linger, hold back, draw her with him. But when she cried out his name, he was lost in her, in all that she offered.

She might die with the pleasure, Maggie thought. Oh, she was glad, really glad, that he had wanted to do this again.

She arched against his touch. With a tracing of his tongue, he roused her until the storm brewing within her exploded with full force. As his fingers played with a master's touch, his mouth spread nibbling kisses downward. Her skin quivered, and pleasure, unbearable pleasure, rose within her. Then with a slowness that threatened to drive her to madness, he entered her. She clung to him, an urgency gripping at her. Arms and legs tangled together. This was more than she'd ever expected, more than she thought possible. Different or not, here, they were one. Here, they moved in unison.

Hazy sunlight streamed into the bedroom. Burying her face against his shoulder, Maggie touched his chest. His breathing was slow, even. So different from the ragged roughness she'd heard hours ago.

Snuggling closer, she kissed his chest and listened to the steady thudding of his heart. She'd never gone out with a man quite as good-looking as him. She recalled talk among friends about Kirsten Elliot Scott and Brady McQueen. He'd always been considered a great catch. And she had him. By some fluke of an idea, she had Brady McQueen as her husband. And she wished she could stay with him like this forever.

No, that wasn't what she really meant, was it? A thread of panic wove its way through her from her own thought. She meant she loved the way she felt at this moment. Warm. Secure. Womanly in his arms. Tell it like it is, she berated herself. She felt desired.

As he stirred, she wondered how long they had before Conor awakened. Unlike other newlyweds, they had a toddler who would rouse full of energy and hungry. "Do you want a big breakfast?"

"Coffee will do." Brady curled a hand around her hip. "I thought you couldn't cook."

"I was thinking about cereal."

Tangled in the cover, he shifted and chuckled in her ear. "Cereal works for me."

She released a whispery laugh. "What about Conor? Doesn't he need more?"

"We're easy to please." He framed her face with his hands and drew it close. Sweet and innocent as she was, she'd been eager, willing, responsive. He doubted she knew the depth of her sensuality. But surely she knew that she'd made him tremble. Content because of her nearness, he dodged pondering what he'd felt earlier. Sunshine and warmth were with him. This woman was light in the dark places of his world.

Maggie was grateful that he'd never murmured any vows to her even during the heat of desire. "I feel wonderful," she said, caressing his ribs.

Eyes closed again, he kissed her shoulder, inhaled her scent, a familiar fragrance now.

"That isn't smart, is it?" she asked softly.

"Don't analyze."

It was her nature to do just that. "I mean—well I could get pregnant."

He felt a catch inside him at the thought. "I'll be more careful next time."

"Or I could get birth control pills." Though it went against her cautious nature, she really didn't want to think too much about anything except how Brady made her feel.

So she told herself later while she carried breakfast dishes to the sink that she was having an affair, a wonderful affair. Nothing more.

Satisfied with such rational thinking, she felt her nerves easing. Her doubts and fears had vanished, too. So what if they were sleeping together? So what if they were playing house? He'd wanted her, and at first, they'd needed each other to make this plan successful. Now, she would admit, that those needs defined too simply what she felt whenever he touched her. She ached for him.

This was about sex, she reasoned. She could enjoy all of this, because she knew love was something intangible that didn't really exist. When the time came to separate, all she would be giving up was the lust she felt for him. The body, not the heart, would have to endure withdrawal. She could deal with that.

What she would never forget was that in her family marriage never worked. Like her parents, she would fail. But unlike them, she would never be responsible for causing a child pain.

Dipping her hands in the dishwater, she stared out the kitchen window. Beneath, bright sunlight grass glistened with moisture. A jackrabbit stopped in the middle of the street curious about a boy on a bike. The mailman paused at the end of the walk and checked the mail, then deposited it in Brady's box. Some of it might be for her.

She dried her hands on a towel before she dashed outside. To simplify her life, she'd given her address and phone number to several friends, contractors for her grandfather's house, her mother, all the members of the historical group, plus a few acquaintances with the animal society she belonged to.

One letter was for her.

Brady played a penguin game with Conor, read him a book, then settled him in front of the television to watch a movie about mice rescuing a little girl.

Able to keep an eye on his son from the kitchen doorway, he wandered toward it to see if Maggie needed help with the dishes. Having her play house-keeper for him and Conor wasn't part of the bargain.

Instead of standing at the sink, she was sitting on a chair, an envelope in her lap. Her stillness bothered him as much as the lost look on her face.

Quickly he moved to her, but even as he squatted before her, he doubted she was seeing him. "Maggie?" He slipped his hand over hers. A second passed, then another before she raised her gaze to his. "What's wrong?"

"A wedding gift." She stared down at the envelope in her lap for a moment. As if it took effort, she handed it to him. "From my mother." He heard raw emotion in her voice. "A check. Her social secretary wrote it. My mother signed it. I doubt that she ever saw the card. I don't know why I expected more.''

More? Brady eyed the figures on the check and thought her mother had been overly generous.

''But then, she couldn't see fit to squeeze my wedding into her life.''

You can't buy love, lady, or alleviate guilt with it, he mused, realizing that's exactly what her mother must have been attempting to do.

Maggie shook her head. ''I haven't seen her in seven years.'' She gave her head another shake as if to banish some thought. ''You'd think by now that I wouldn't expect more from her. After all, she didn't even come back to the States when my grandfather died.''

More than disgust rippled through him. Anger for this sweet, caring woman filled him.

''She was never near when I needed her.''

Letting go of her hand, he cupped her chin and angled her face toward his. He saw the wetness in her eyes. She wouldn't want someone to see her cry, but he wasn't just anyone. For as long as it took to accomplish their goals, he was her husband, and he planned to be a damn good one. Drawing her into his arms, he felt her stiffen. Deliberately, he kept his voice soft because she seemed to be teetering on the edge of too many emotions. ''I'm here for you.'' Brady held her, waiting for her to relax against him. ''You're more of a mother to Conor than she'll ever be for you.''

Maggie took a deep breath and drew back to look at him.

"She's not a mother, Maggie. She'll probably never be."

"Do I just pretend that she doesn't exist?"

"Do whatever you have to that won't make you feel sad," he said softly. "She's not worth your tears."

"I don't usually think about her but—times like this, I don't want to see her again. That's what I feel, and that's wrong."

"Why is it wrong?" With a fingertip, he brushed strands of hair away from her cheek. "You have nothing to ever feel guilty about."

"I don't love her," she said, letting words she'd never said to anyone slip out.

"Love has to be deserved."

Wearily she sighed.

"I can't expect Conor to love me if I don't show him how much I love him." He pressed his lips to her forehead. "Don't cry anymore for her." Silently he called her mother names. How, he wondered, could a woman walk away from her child?

"I'm okay now." Maggie drew an uneven breath and delivered an equally shaky smile.

"Yes, you are. You're better than okay," he said, with admiration for her strength. This fragile-looking, sweet woman possessed a resilience that he could never imagine having.

"Hello," a cheery voice called out from the other room. "I'm home."

Tensing, Maggie jerked back. "Renie?"

The questions in her eyes eased away some of the anguish. "Renie," Brady answered.

Quickly Maggie brushed at her wet cheeks. "Do I look all right?"

"You always look wonderful to me." He meant that, and knew it was wrong.

Maggie gave him a wry grin. "That's not what I meant."

"You look fine," he assured her.

"Look who I got a big hug from," Renie said, appearing in the doorway and holding Conor.

Maggie rose and forced a bright smile. From what Brady had told her about his housekeeper, she would be the hardest person to fool. She'd become more than an employee; she was a friend, part of the family.

"So this is your new wife," Renie said with warmth and enthusiasm. "Hello, Mrs. McQueen."

"Hi." Maggie caught the amused look on Brady's face at the woman's formality. Obviously that wasn't normal for her. "Would you call me Maggie?"

A softer light came into the woman's eyes. "Okay, Maggie."

Maggie wanted the woman to like her, but Renie had been a part of Kirsten's life. And she was so different from Brady's first wife.

"You," she was saying to Brady, "are still in the doghouse for getting married when I wasn't here."

As Renie sent Maggie a discreet but curious look, Maggie inwardly cringed. Close to Brady, could Renie sense that this wasn't a marriage based on love?

Brady watched his wife putting on her best face. Never again did he want to hear such sadness in her voice. How had someone who'd suffered so much become such a caring person? Instinctively he drew her closer, aware he wanted to protect her from any kind of hurt, especially from him. "As long as you're home, Renie, want to baby-sit? It'll give you another night out of the kitchen. I thought Maggie and I would go out to eat." He glanced at his wife. "Want to? Someplace romantic," he added with a grin.

Maggie assumed the words, the grin and the wink at her were for Renie's benefit. "I'd love to," she said, with a smile that she hoped conveyed a loving wife wanting to be alone with her husband.

Maggie expected dinner at an exquisite restaurant frequented by acquaintances of theirs. The restaurant he chose was Italian, intimate, romantic, filled with wonderful aromas, flickering candles and a violinist playing dreamy music.

Maggie saw no one they knew.

She looked enchanting, Brady thought not for the first time. The pale blue, sleeveless silk dress drew his attention to her blue eyes. Since their marriage, she'd revamped her wardrobe with a few more evening clothes. He thought he liked this dress the best on her.

"They know you here?" Maggie asked, recalling the warm welcome of the restaurant's owner, a thin man with a thick accent.

"You don't like it?" he asked with concern. He knew she would never find anyone from the Junior League dining at the family-owned restaurant, but besides the enjoyment of the good food, he'd always liked the cozy atmosphere.

"I like it," Maggie replied, quick to answer.

"Good." He couldn't stop himself from saying what he was thinking. "I wanted to be alone with you," he said softly, letting his fingers skim the top of her hand resting on the table.

Despite her previous intimacy with him, the mere touch of his fingers heated her. Still uncertain about how to deal with the feelings he aroused within her, she searched for conversation. "About my apartment—"

Brady looked up from the wine in his glass. "You have to let it go." He hated to ask that of her, because he knew she was sacrificing more than he was, but he thought she needed a reminder. "If you don't do it, your cousin will have ammunition. Her lawyer can say that you kept the apartment because you knew you'd be moving back to it shortly."

There was too much truth in what he'd said for her to argue, but she'd been stalling. That was such a final move, and when this ended between her and Brady, where would she live? "When I leave—"

"You can take your time," he cut in. "You don't have to rush from my place." He couldn't explain the feeling of annoyance washing over him. He would be alone again, raising Conor. He wouldn't smell her fragrance on the pillowcase. He would be alone again in that bed. Oh, he knew that was his choice. There were women, enough of them. If he wanted to play that kind of game, he never had to spend a night alone. But the thought of bringing another woman into his house, into that bed, was suddenly unthinkable. He couldn't imagine anyone in it except her.

"You looked surprised when Renie called me Mrs. McQueen."

Brady made a concentrated effort to dodge his last thought. "I shouldn't have been."

"Why? Because she's not convinced?"

Brady wondered if she knew how classically beautiful she looked. "No." He curled his fingers around her hand. She was so delicate, he thought, noting how pale her skin looked against his. "Kirsten insisted on being called that. You pleased Renie," he assured her. He watched candlelight play across her face. "She can put out a top-notch formal dinner, but deep down, she's rough around the edges."

"Which is why you like her?"

"She suited me better than she did Kirsten. Do you like her?"

"I think so. I hope she gives me a chance to find out."

"Why wouldn't she?"

Because her loyalty is probably still with the first wife. "I really don't think she's convinced."

"There's no reason for her not to be."

Maggie thought he wasn't thinking clearly. She was wrong for him. She was nothing like Kirsten or other women he had had in his life. "About earlier," Maggie began, seeing no purpose in pressing her point. "I'm sorry I lost it today," she said, uncomfortable about crying in front of him.

Don't retreat now, Brady wanted to yell. "We're friends, aren't we?"

Maggie nearly blushed. They were closer than that. "That, too," she admitted, amazed how close she'd gotten to him in such a short time.

He gave her that irresistible grin of his. "Yeah, that, too." Brady did what he'd wanted to do for hours. Lightly, he framed her face with his hand and pressed his mouth to hers. Like her scent, her taste enticed him. "Don't ever be afraid to show your feelings. Not with me," he said softly.

She hadn't known him before, Maggie acknowledged. She hadn't known his undefinable gentleness with his son, the intensity of his desire, his sweet thoughtfulness when he'd thought he'd hurt her the first time, or his compassion earlier when she'd fallen apart.

No, she hadn't known him. Hadn't known she could feel this close to any man.

Chapter Ten

After five days away from home, Brady had dashed from the hotel and a press conference with the basketball coaches to a taxi to catch the earlier flight home. Now he sat in the airport terminal twiddling his thumbs because of a delay. The days and nights had been hell because he'd missed his son, he'd told himself, but whenever he'd called home and had heard Maggie's voice, he'd known that part of the emptiness within him was because of her.

Growing impatient, he weaved a path to the telephone. While married to Kirsten, she'd insisted on him phoning before he boarded the plane, as if she'd needed reassurance he was on the way home. Now he was the one needing reassurance.

People hurried to or waited for a plane. A woman fed her baby its bottle. A hand-holding elderly couple, still dressed in flowery Miami vacation clothes, kissed. A young couple wrapped arms around each other. Love was everywhere. Inside him, too. He was falling in love with Maggie.

And hell, that wouldn't do.

Margaret Buchanan had never missed any man, except her grandfather and brother. By the time she'd turned ten, she'd viewed separations from her parents as a fact of life. Prior to her marriage, she'd never been close enough to anyone to reach for someone in the middle of the night, to be aware of a man's whistling as he came from the bathroom after a shower, to listen for a child's cry from the next room.

But Maggie McQueen was counting the hours until her husband came home from the road trip. A husband in name only, she tried to remind herself. That's all Brady was supposed to be, but sleeping with a man tightened an emotional strap around a woman that Maggie had never expected.

So here she was anticipating Brady's return home from Miami.

His phone call last night and another this morning had helped. She assumed he'd been checking on Conor. "Sticky," she said to his son now, and wiped Conor's fingers.

He hand-delivered the last canned pear to his mouth. "Sticky," he repeated.

"Yes, you're sticky," Maggie agreed, smiling.

At the sink behind her, Renie chuckled. "He'll be yakking nonstop soon."

Over her shoulder, Maggie matched the woman's smile. "He does a good job of communicating now."

The ring of the telephone overshadowed her last word.

Sounding every bit as intimidating as Herta, the maid Maggie had known in her youth, Renie answered, "The McQueen residence. Oh, sure," she said in her more normal, easy tone a second later. "Brady." She held the receiver toward Maggie.

Maggie stood torn as Conor raised his arms to her. "I'll wash him up," Renie volunteered.

Maggie cuddled Conor for a second, then made the exchange with Renie. "Hello," she said as Renie, on her way to the doorway, nuzzled Conor's neck, making him giggle.

"It's me," Brady said.

Maggie switched the phone to her other ear. "Is there a problem? This is your third call."

The problem was how much he'd missed the sound of her voice. "No problem." Brady braced a shoulder against the wall beside the phone. "I wanted to make sure you were both okay. I guess—" He hesitated. "I miss you," he said honestly, unable to stop himself.

Maggie sank to the closest chair. When he'd said he wanted her, that had been easy to accept. Sex with someone could be viewed as a noncommittal kind of relationship, though she'd already felt more feelings than desire for him. For him to say what she'd been feeling edged dangerously close to a commitment.

With Maggie's silence, Brady turned his back on the noise in the airport terminal. Was she thinking of ways to distance herself? Had her back stiffened in self-defense to the emotion that accompanied those words?

"Brady?"

"Yeah."

"We miss you, too." There, she'd said it, but she was already wondering if she'd made a mistake.

He was pleased. "I'll see you soon."

"Bye." She waited for the dial tone, then set down the receiver. Her heart still thudded with excitement.

By late afternoon, Maggie couldn't stop clock watching, waiting for Brady's phone call from the airport so she could leave and pick him up. On her knees, with sand under her trim, well-manicured nails as she played in the sandbox with Conor, she faced the obvious. She was letting emotion for both of them pull her in deeper and deeper with each passing day.

"You do," Conor said, raising eyes filled with expectation up to her.

Maggie grabbed a spoon to join him in filling a bucket with sand. "Conor, you do it, too," she said when she noticed he'd stopped to let her complete the task, but his attention had shifted elsewhere.

"Da," he shouted.

Maggie followed his bright-eyed stare. Standing at the back door, Brady looked absolutely wonderful to her. Something definitely was happening. That she yearned to feel herself in his arms, that she almost scrambled to her feet and rushed to him signaled the dangerous feelings developing within her. It took effort to remind herself that they were only playing house. "Hi." Smiling, she rose slowly and watched Conor scurry to his father.

"Hi, yourself." Brady dragged his gaze from her

and looked down as Conor plowed into his legs. "Hey, sport."

Conor released a delighted squeal when Brady caught him under the arms and lifted him above his head. "Da."

As Brady hugged him, he felt one of his son's little hands tapping affectionately on his back.

"You should have called," Maggie said, stepping near to them. "I would have picked you up at the airport."

He wanted to pull her close with his other arm. "You look—"

Maggie laughed and self-consciously rubbed her dirty palms down denim-clad thighs. "A mess."

"Good to me."

The softness in his voice moved over her like a caress. "And you look tired. You didn't sleep well?"

"Lousy." The scent that had taunted him while he'd been away drifted over him now.

"Bad mattress?"

His eyes never leaving hers, he reached out and caught a strand of her hair.

No matter what her good sense told her, Maggie couldn't stop what she felt. She slid her hand from his waist to his back as he bent his head and kissed her neck.

Roaming light kisses now along her jaw to her cheek, Brady felt the serenity that had been missing for the past day—because his son hadn't been near, because she hadn't. "I wanted to get home," he whispered against her ear. "That's all I could think about." The admittance came out mumbled. It wasn't time to talk. The sweetness he'd craved was near. He plunged one hand into her hair and pressed his mouth hard against hers. At the moment, all he wanted was to keep her close, to be a part of her again.

With his arm still around her and Conor snuggled against him, they walked into the house. Maggie had always believed she was immune to these emotions, but she hadn't known how wonderful it felt to be a part of something so special, to have people who cared about her.

While Renie prepared lunch, Maggie cleaned up Conor. At the sound of Brady's voice in his study, she assumed he was on the phone and took her time changing Conor's clothes.

"Shews," he said, pointing to one of his.

"Yes, shoes. I'll get these tied and you can eat."

"No."

Maggie smiled. In the last few days that word had consistently crept into conversations with him. "Okay, don't eat."

"No," he said again.

Maggie laughed and hugged him to her. Little arms curled around her neck, hard. "I love you, Conor."

"Uve you," he repeated.

In less time than it took to take a breath, something twisted and moved within her. Maggie shut her eyes. Here was all she could ask for in unconditional love. She kept Conor close a moment longer. An urge to cry still threatened, knotting her throat, tightening her chest. She would pay a price when she had to leave, she knew now, and took another second to pull herself together.

"Are you two ready for lunch?" Brady called, then appeared in the doorway.

"Eat," Conor shouted with enthusiasm and barreled toward his father.

"I called my mother," Brady said when Maggie joined him and Conor in the hallway. He'd told her everything, including the love within him for his wife.

"You told her the truth?"

Brady slipped an arm around Maggie's shoulder. "I told her."

"How did she take the news about the arrangement?" she asked with concern.

He held her closer a moment longer to kiss the frown line between her brows. "She wished me luck." Her scent drifting over him, she clouded his brain. His conscience told him he shouldn't love her, but right now he wanted every second he could have with her.

Lunch proved noisy. Conor bellowed his protest at not getting cookies for his meal. Renie jabbered about a friend who'd started in-line skating and would probably end up with a broken leg. Maggie coaxed Conor to eat his lunch and periodically shared with Brady what she did yesterday while he'd been gone. Brady loved every minute.

Even before they finished eating, Conor grew crabby with tiredness. Soothing him with an off-key rendition of "Row, Row, Row Your Boat," Brady carried his sleepy son to his room.

Maggie finished helping Renie clean up, then a few moments later strolled down the hallway. Slowing her stride, she viewed the room next to Brady's study. With a floor-to-ceiling window, the room was centered around a big-screen television, but there were

two other smaller sets in a far corner near one cush-
iony sofa. The first time she'd seen the room, she'd
laughed. A basketball hoop hung above the doorway,
a pool table stretched almost half the length of the
room. A video game unit occupied a far corner, along
with a golf bag and clubs. Several rackets for various
sports hung on a far wall. It was an adolescent boy's
dream room.

"Want to play pool?" Brady asked behind her.

Maggie gave up her interest in what she assumed
most males would view as nirvana. "I don't know
how."

"I'll teach you." Her back to him, he took her by
the shoulders and directed her toward the pool table.
"If Charlie can play, you can," he added with a
good-natured laugh.

Maggie glanced at the galley clock on the wall
above a dartboard. At home, she'd always allotted this
time of the day for relaxing and listening to music.
"On one condition." She stepped away and wandered
to the cabinet where she'd stored several of her CDs.

Brady veiled a grin. He liked the way she chal-
lenged him. "What is it?"

She held up a CD. "We listen to this while we
play pool."

He couldn't help it; he laughed. Usually his background music leaned toward smooth jazz. "Mozart?"

Maggie waited for his gaze to return to hers.
"Okay?"

Anything you want, he mused. "Okay."

"There are fifteen balls," Maggie said, having already counted them. "What's the white one?"

"The cue ball?" Brady racked the balls. "Here."

He stepped behind her. "Hold the stick like this," he said, with his arms bordering hers as he positioned her fingers on the stick.

Maggie sent him a look over her shoulder. "I'll never concentrate if you stay like this."

Grinning, Brady stepped back. "Bothered you, huh?"

Maggie veiled a smile. "Don't let it go to your head," she teased back.

She gave him another one of those dynamite smiles of hers, then sank a ball in a side pocket. "I moved a few of my things over here while you were gone, but I need to get the rest," Maggie said, stretching across the table as she eyed the next ball.

Balls clattered. Another one thudded in a corner pocket.

"We can go later to your apartment."

"When Conor awakens." She had no idea what she should keep, what she should put in storage. "I guess it's your turn."

Leaning on his stick, Brady had enjoyed himself. "Thanks for giving me a chance."

A tease sparkling in her eyes, she swept an arm toward the table. "Do your best."

Still at arm's length from her, he reached forward and slipped a hand at the nape of her neck, then slowly drew her to him. "I always do," he murmured as he inclined his head to kiss her.

"I can leave the furniture," Maggie said while Brady helped her pack a box with books.

Brady watched her frown. When they'd first arrived at her apartment, she'd been stymied about what to do with her piano, until he'd insisted it be moved to the house. But what about her books, the collection of Baccarat crystal in a curio cabinet? This was unfair to her, Brady realized. He'd asked her to move into his home, abandon her own and accept his choice of furniture and decor. Women liked stamping a house with their own touch—little knickknacks, a special painting, a favorite teapot or coffee cup.

"Pepi?" Conor asked while tugging on the leg of Brady's jeans.

"No soft drink." Slanting a look at Maggie bent over and packing another box with the books, Brady pleasurably took a lengthy view of the denim straining across her backside. For the fun of the moment, when she swiveled a look over her shoulder at him, he let his eyes sweep down her body, not bothering to hide exactly where his thoughts had wandered.

Maggie responded to his grin with an amused smile. "There's juice in the refrigerator for Conor."

"You're good at that," he teased.

She closed the flaps on a carton. "At what?"

"Sidetracking."

Maggie released a soft laugh. "Get his juice."

Brady thought of how often he'd heard her laughter lately. For both of them, the rules of the marriage bargain had altered. While she'd been reluctant at first, he felt none of that or her wariness now. For him, he'd found more than he'd hoped for, more than he had a right to have.

In the kitchen, he flung open the refrigerator door and started to reach for the juice. There was no one else like her, he thought as he removed two flower bulbs. "What are these?" he asked, holding them out to her.

Maggie shoved a box toward the others and looked up. "Tulip bulbs. For planting in spring."

"Where do you want me to pack them?"

Maggie shrugged. Whoever took over her apartment wouldn't want them, and what if she lost her grandfather's house? Why was she saving them? "Toss them in the garbage can."

Brady handed Conor a cup with a lid and a straw. "Maggie, there's room in the refrigerator at home. And don't tell me you don't want those," he said, indicating her crystal. Or that," he added, motioning toward a well-cared-for hanging plant.

Maggie eyed her philodendron. "Where would I put it?"

"Wherever you want," he said as he closed the distance to her to take a carton from her arms. "It's your home, too."

Home. Maggie had never really known a home of any kind until she'd lived with her grandparents. But even before Brady had said those words to her, she'd begun to feel that way about his house. It had nothing to do with her possessions. It was because of him and Conor. Sure, she knew now where everything was, but the feeling came from the way she felt, from something as simple as pouring bubbles into the bathwater for Conor, she realized later.

Done with dinner, she knelt beside the bathtub and watched him. On his belly, he alternated between swimming in the few inches of bathwater and making zooming noises while he pushed his boat around the water.

A sense of home didn't come from a place, but a feeling.

That was why her grandfather's home had meant so much to her. She'd wanted to preserve the house where she'd felt love.

"Cold?" she questioned Conor as he shivered. His little fingers looked shriveled from the lengthy time in the bathwater.

"Tol," he answered.

Smiling, Maggie wrapped a towel around him. He smelled sweeter than any flower. Hugging him, she wondered how long it would take to forget, to not yearn for a second of such a moment after she and Brady ended their marriage. Maggie stroked Conor's soft hair, then kissed the top of his head. She would miss the little boy snuggling in her arms as if she were special to him. She would miss him for a long time, she realized as he wrapped little arms around her neck and lovingly tightened them.

Holding on to him, she dropped his toy boat, sudsy from the bubbles in the sink, and turned on the cold water. It rushed over the boat, rinsing away the suds. It also seeped into her socks. Looking down, she stared at the water oozing out from under the sink cabinet.

Squatting, Maggie whipped open the cabinet and got a faceful of water. She released a mental curse, then snatched several towels from behind her and dropped them on the floor. "Brady," she yelled, then gave a start as he appeared in the doorway sooner than she anticipated.

He laughed. "What?" His voice trailed off as his eyes flicked from the dripping strands of her hair to the soaked towels on the floors. "What in the...?"

"A pipe under the sink is leaking."

In the close confines of the bathroom, he touched her hip to move in while she stepped out with a towel-wrapped Conor.

"Can you fix it?"

In typical male fashion, he slanted a look of disbelief at her. "I'm a man. We can fix anything."

"Oh." Stifling her grin, she left with Conor, but several times while she was diapering and dressing him in pajamas, she heard Brady release a lusty curse. Holding Conor in her arms, she ambled back to the bathroom and leaned against the doorjamb. On the floor, his head under the sink, Brady muttered an even more explicit expletive. "I could call a plumber," Maggie suggested.

He returned a predictable macho answer. "I'll fix it."

"Don't you have to work in your study?"

"Already turned in my column."

As the wrench clanged against a pipe, Maggie set Conor down. "Wawr," he announced while squatting in front of the cabinet and pointing at the stream squirting from the pipe in an arc from the cabinet and onto the floor.

"Yes, water," Maggie responded. She grabbed an old towel from the nearby linen closet and dropped it onto the puddle. "I'll get a mop," she said, and winced as she heard another, more mumbled curse from under the sink.

It was the final one, it seemed. Within seconds,

Brady placed his hands on the sink cabinet to pull himself out from under it. When his head popped out, Maggie smiled and handed him a towel.

It masked everything but his eyes, smiling at her.

"Broke?" his son asked, still engrossed in the pipes under the sink.

"Nope. All fixed," Brady assured him while he ran the towel over his damp forearms. "At least, it better be." His voice trailed off in response to the slam of a door.

"Anyone home?" Bennett's voice boomed from another room before he came down the hallway toward the bathroom. "Renie let me in," he said, stopping beside Maggie. Amusement sparkling in his eyes, he swept a look over the mess on the bathroom floor. "You do pick the strangest places to have parties, McQueen."

In retaliation, Brady tossed a damp towel at Bennett's face.

Grabbing it before the cloth hit its target, Bennett laughed.

"Ben," Conor said gleefully.

Looking pleased at the greeting, Bennett smacked a kiss on Conor's cheek. "Hi, big guy."

Despite her brother's teasing and smiles, Maggie read concern in his eyes. When his gaze remained on Brady, she gathered he was the one Bennett had come to see. She prayed he hadn't come with a custody problem. "If you'll all get out of here, I'll clean this up," she urged, nudging Bennett's shoulder to maneuver him out of the doorway. She also planned a nice, long shower for herself.

"Bossy," Bennett teased. "She's been like that since she was little."

Maggie aimed a departing, withering glance at him.

"That definitely was a homey little scene," Bennett said as he trailed Brady to the living room. "Too bad I can't offer the court my opinion."

Brady set Conor down. Annoyance skittered through him at the reminder that the marriage wasn't real. He didn't want a reminder. With each day that had passed, the original agreement between Maggie and him had become less clear-cut.

Bennett dropped onto the sofa and chuckled as Conor bent over in the start of a headstand. "Going to the party Saturday night?"

"Party?" Brady narrowed questioning eyes at him. He was so caught up in what was happening between him and Maggie, spending time with his son and keeping pace with work that he'd lost sight of the goings-on of the outside world. "Halloween."

"You got it." Bennett rested back against the arm of the sofa. "It's a must that you two go. It's a high-profile-type event."

Brady thought just the opposite. "How did you come to that conclusion? Everyone will be in disguise. Masquerade parties mean wearing masks."

"Absolutely." Bennett inclined his head. "What's your problem? You always liked parties."

He didn't want to be with other people. There was something comforting about being alone with Maggie and Conor, about being together like a family. "I told you why. It doesn't make sense to go if no one will know we're there."

"Everyone will know," Bennett responded.

"You've been to other masquerade parties that the country club has held. Everyone tries to guess who's who. So everyone is aware who is there."

Brady knew his friend was right. "Okay, we'll be there. What we're going to wear—" He paused and shrugged.

"Something that keeps people guessing would work."

"At the last minute like this, we'll probably end up with something dumb like Tweety Bird and Sylvester the Cat."

Bennett chuckled and pushed to his feet. "That would be worth seeing."

Showered, Maggie tied her robe tight and left the bathroom to the sound of male laughter and wandered back to the living room in time to see Bennett leaving.

"See you Saturday," he called out from the doorway.

She sent Brady a puzzled look. "Saturday?"

"The masquerade party," Brady explained. He waited until they were alone. "He came by to remind us that we should go."

"We don't have any costumes."

"We'd better hope we can still rent something." He laughed against the fresh, clean scent of her hair. "You smell wonderful." Certain that after carting in her boxes he carried the raunchy odors of a locker room, he stepped back. "I'll go shower. But don't forget where we were."

Forget? How could she? Amazingly, they'd been intimate, and she still felt a giddy thrill whenever he touched or kissed her. In weeks he'd turned her world topsy-turvy. Hadn't she begun to act strangely, no longer scheduling her day? But instead of feeling displeasure, she smiled at that thought. A two-year-old did have a unique talent at thwarting plans of any kind. Conor had become as much of an influence in her life as Brady had.

A smile still tugged at her lips when the doorbell rang seconds later. Out of habit from living alone most of her adult life, Maggie strolled to the window to see who the caller was. A familiar face glared back at her.

Olivia didn't wait for an invitation after Maggie opened the door. With her chauffeur waiting in the foyer, she strode toward the living room, head up, her cane tapping softly on the foyer's oak floor. Her eyes swept the living room and stopped at the sight of an antique blue glass duck candy dish. "That," she said, gesturing with her cane, "belonged to my daughter. Do you enjoy living in a house filled with the memories and possessions of another woman?"

Maggie hadn't allowed herself to think about what had belonged to another woman. "Did you want to see Brady?" She noted that Conor, playing nearby with a puzzle, hadn't looked up. More important, Olivia hadn't greeted him.

"No, I did not. I thought you might act rational and admit that this marriage is an immense farce."

Maggie remained quiet. Why had she and Brady believed that no one would question the motives behind their quick marriage? They seemed to have fooled no one.

"By your silence, I gather you plan on playing the fool about him just as my daughter did."

Maggie turned her attention to Conor. The woman

claimed she wanted him, yet she still hadn't even reached out to him.

"You can tell him that I made a promise. I vow to use every penny I possess to win full custody of my grandson. He belongs with me, not his father, not the man responsible for his mother's death."

Maggie felt the blood drain from her.

"Did he forget to mention that?"

Don't pay attention to her, Maggie told herself. *She's vindictive, mean-spirited. She would do anything to hurt Brady.*

"I can see that you don't believe me."

Maggie didn't hesitate. "No, I don't." She'd gotten to know the man Kirsten had loved. He was kind and gentle. He was loving and caring.

Reaching out, Olivia started to touch Conor's head.

He dodged her hand. "No!" he insisted defiantly, his little chin thrusting up stubbornly. "Move." He pushed at her hand to shove it away from him.

As if poked, Olivia's back stiffened. "He's quite unmanageable now, I see. But he won't be for very long. He is the son of Kirsten Elliot Scott. He will be raised accordingly. He will become a proper young gentleman."

Maggie felt the heat of temper rise within her. "He's a McQueen, too," she calmly reminded the woman. "He needs his father."

Her attention elsewhere, Olivia bellowed a demand. "No!"

Startled, Conor jerked his hand back as if the glass duck he'd started to touch held the heat of fire.

"Bad boy!" Olivia yelled.

Maggie intervened. "Now, wait a minute."

"Intolerable. Absolutely intolerable behavior," Olivia insisted, and gestured with her cane at her chauffeur. He moved forward on cue. "I'm taking this home," she said, snatching the duck from the shelf and handing it to the man. "And you!" She pointed a finger at Conor. "You will be disciplined when you are home again. Now, come here."

"He is home," Maggie countered.

"Not for long."

Maggie didn't bother to argue.

As Olivia reached for Conor's arm to drag him closer, he wailed.

"Stop that!" Olivia yelled.

He yanked free of her, sat on the floor and howled.

Her face pinched, Olivia clapped her hands. "Stop that!"

His cry growing louder, he kicked his little legs out in front of him.

Maggie had never seen him like that.

Olivia swung away. "Already he's showing signs of lacking discipline," she said over Conor's crying. "He needs the firm hand of an English nanny."

Maggie started to reach for Conor. In what appeared an inconsolable move, he scrambled away and moved to a corner, turning his back on both of them. Maggie's heart ached for him. As a child, she had known the firm, almost inhibiting manner of a strict nanny. Sit properly, be still. She'd often been reprimanded for the tiniest speck of dirt on her clothing.

"My grandchild will not be dragged up like some common street urchin by his father."

Maggie let Olivia's exaggeration roll off her. Not

waiting until the door closed behind her, she knelt beside Conor.

Tears still streamed down his cheeks. His little shoulders shook with sobs. "Hold."

Her heart aching for him, Maggie rocked him as much to soothe herself as him. He was a good-natured child who laughed and smiled often. He would resort to withdrawal if forced to live in Olivia's rigid lifestyle.

"I overheard," Renie said, standing near. "Brady wasn't responsible for her daughter's death. She won't accept who her daughter was."

Maggie stroked Conor's hair. Sensing an ally, she urged more from Renie. "Why don't you tell me?"

"Can't." She turned on her heels to return to the kitchen.

Maggie followed. "This is between us," she promised, taking a tissue from her pocket to wipe tears from Conor's eyes.

Renie waited while Maggie got Conor interested in his building blocks in a corner of the room. "You know why Brady thinks he needs to call you so often when he's away? *She* insisted on it."

"She? You mean Kirsten?" Maggie asked with a look over her shoulder.

Renie busied herself at the sink.

"Renie?" Maggie caught Renie's arm to halt her movement. "I thought we'd become friends."

Renie dropped the sponge she held into the sudsy dishwater. "We are, but—"

"What is it you're not telling me?"

"She especially made him call before he boarded

the plane. He thought she needed reassurance he was on his way home.''

''That wasn't true?''

''She wasn't without flaws. I don't know why he keeps forgetting that.''

Because he feels guilty about her death. ''She was unfaithful?''

''During the last month, yes. She was like a different person. But then she was drinking a lot more and always popping pills into her mouth. I told her to be careful.''

''You knew?'' Maggie frowned. Why hadn't she told Brady?

''So did Mrs. Olivia Elliot Scott. She said it was Brady's fault her daughter needed the pills. That was a lie. Who do you think had the influence to keep getting her daughter's prescriptions refilled? When I said something to her about it, she said Kirsten needed them to *calm* her.''

''But she died from mixing those prescriptions with alcohol? It was an accident, wasn't it?''

''Sure it was, but she was a substance abuser,'' Renie said firmly. ''Even if he had known, she wouldn't have listened to him, or stopped. I tried. I told Mrs. McQueen I had to tell Brady before she hurt herself. She told me to keep my trap shut. Her words.'' Renie arched a brow. ''She wasn't such a grand lady all the time.'' She wiped the towel hard across her damp hands. ''She told me if I said anything, I'd be gone.'' Some of the anger slipped from Renie's voice. ''What would happen to Conor then? Kirsten wouldn't watch him. She was too busy running around.''

Sadness overwhelmed Maggie. How could she ever spoil Brady's memory of Kirsten with the truth?

"So you can see. I couldn't say what I knew." Her voice trailed off as her eyes looked past Maggie.

A tenseness knotted Maggie's stomach even before she turned, before she saw Brady standing in the doorway.

Chapter Eleven

Stunned. It was the only word to describe the look on Brady's face. He'd heard everything, Maggie realized.

"All this time I thought—"

Renie sighed heavily. "I'm sorry."

Maggie felt miserable for him. He took several deep breaths, as if even that was difficult, then he turned away. She wanted to go to him, hold him. And say what? she wondered. He was hurting. Memories were tarnished suddenly.

"Oh, Maggie," Renie said softly.

"It'll be all right," she said to ease the woman's concern. She hoped she was right. Looking down at Conor, she saw him yawn. "Night-night," she said before she steered Conor toward the bedroom. Cuddling him, a part of Brady, made her feel momentarily useful.

Conor was asleep in minutes. A peacefulness had returned to his face. Maggie drew the blanket with its baseball design over Conor's shoulders, then pressed her lips to the top of Conor's head before heading toward Brady's and her bedroom to find him. Whatever it took, she would do it to keep Conor from that woman. Conor could be hurt badly if Brady didn't win final custody of him.

Barefoot and head bent while he tied his robe, Brady wandered out of the bathroom. While alone, he'd thought back to the days—months—after Kirsten's death. He'd believed he'd been so oblivious, so self-absorbed that he'd missed all the indicators she was in trouble. But from what Renie had said, he'd never really known the woman he'd married. For four years, he'd loved her, touched every inch of her, yet she'd been a stranger to him.

Maggie saw pain in his eyes. "Don't be angry at Renie. I'm sure if she'd known how guilty you felt she would have told you, but—"

"But?" He glanced at her, solemn-looking.

"She thought—she believed you thought Kirsten was perfect. She saw no reason to hurt you with the truth."

No man liked learning he'd been a fool. The woman he'd believed he'd married had been an illusion. "I'm not angry at Renie."

"Brady, if I learned anything through all those terrible years when my parents never came around, it was that we're not responsible for what other people do." Maggie sat on the edge of the bed. "They make their own decisions."

Through his own mental fog, he realized how much

she'd disclosed to him just then. "Did you think what they were doing was your fault?"

"Oh, yes." As he came near, Maggie caught his hand. "What else could I believe? They were fighting over me," she said, looking at him as he sat now shoulder to shoulder with her on the bed. "I must have done something to cause so much anger."

"You were a child. There's a big difference."

The sadness in his voice matched what she saw in his eyes. Maggie touched his arm and waited until he looked at her. "No, there isn't. You've believed you'd done something to cause her death." She ached to help him drift away from tormenting thoughts. She saw the doubts still in his eyes. She wished more than anything in the world that she knew how to reach him, to give him peace. He'd just learned his wife hadn't been the woman he'd thought she was. Give me your pain, Maggie wanted to say. "It wasn't your fault," she said softly, and leaned closer, framing his face with her hand.

Not his fault.

"You can't blame yourself for what she did."

Guilt still poked at him. It hurt a lot less to take the blame. Didn't she understand that? What she was asking him to face was that the person he'd loved had self-destructed without a care about him. As Maggie's arm tightened around him, he fought to see beyond the shadow of his own anguish.

How could memories of Kirsten and their marriage have gotten so cloudy that he'd only allowed himself to remember everything she'd done as perfect? More guilt? The more perfect Kirsten had been in memory, the more he'd blamed himself. But what else could he do? For months, he'd believed he was responsible through neglect for what had happened to her. But that wasn't true, he knew now. When she'd died, she'd been different from the woman he'd fallen in love with and married. The emotion that had been playing through him eased off. He'd been possessed by guilt for so long, too long.

"Brady?"

There was a purity to Maggie's touch. He might never have been able to change what Kirsten had been doing. But he couldn't stop living. Or loving. God, he wanted to love again, be loved by this woman sitting silently beside him. He slid his fingers around Maggie's hand, turned her palm up and kissed it. He wanted everything with her. *I love you.* Simple words, ones she would pull away from. Lowering his lips to hers, he took his fill. Her mouth answered his with a willingness that weakened him. All he could do was treasure her, and every moment with her.

Maggie melted against him when he buried his hand in her hair. His lips wouldn't leave hers. She gave all she could to pull one emotion from him, free him finally of the guilt he'd never really deserved. Give. Pleasure. She savored his taste while she tugged at the tie on his robe in her eagerness to caress him. She didn't wait, couldn't.

As his mouth twisted across hers, she ran her hands over the smooth, muscled planes of his chest. His breath came out hot and caressing on her lips, and a groan slipped from his throat.

Patience thinning, they peeled the robes off each other, as if hungry for the warmth of each other's flesh. When his mouth coursed downward and freely tasted, her skin quivered with a need for more. "Love me," she murmured.

He wanted to tell her how much. Instead, he whispered her name before he scooted down, his mouth grazing the softness of her belly.

Maggie trembled. Like a butterfly's caress, his fingers stroked and played over her. Pleasure skittered through her when his mouth followed the same path. Gripping his shoulders tightly, fiercely, she rode a wave of sensation. She'd drunk nothing, yet felt the light-headedness of intoxication. Her flesh tingled wherever he stroked, wherever he tasted. Trembling, she clung, caught up in his soft caresses, his hot kisses.

Was this the way of love? she wondered, feeling desperate for him. She curled her legs around him. With passion bursting through her, she ran her hands across the muscles of his back. Eyes closed, she arched her back in a gesture of invitation. Even as desire made his touch a little more demanding, as she felt him hard and hot and ready against her, she felt cherished. And she wanted to give that back to him.

Her heart beating quicker, she rose up to draw him to her. She heard him murmur her name. She was his before he slipped into her. As one, they moved, they fed on each other's excitement, and she wondered if such giving was a once-in-a-lifetime moment. Then, on a gasp filled with pleasure, she dived beyond the brink of sanity, and all thoughts tumbled from her mind.

The faint blush of dawn streamed through the venetian blinds. For a long moment, Brady didn't move.

With every breath, he absorbed Maggie's scent on the pillow beside him, in the air. He hadn't realized until his marriage to her how much he'd always enjoyed waking up with a woman. Right now he was alone, and missing her. Easing out of the bed, he grabbed his jeans.

Wearing only them, he padded into the kitchen. She was moving around it with a fluid, swift efficiency. Recalling last night, he remembered how incredibly slowly, sensuously slowly, she'd moved, and how much she'd given him when he'd needed her most.

"Believe it or not, Conor is still sleeping," she said when she saw him in the doorway.

"He takes after his father." With a shoulder braced against the doorjamb, he gave her a smile. This morning seemed different, brighter. Because of her, he realized as he moved close behind her. "He likes to sort of take his time getting out of bed. You should try it sometime."

As his hand came around to rest on her belly, Maggie angled a look back at him. Beneath the hands on her, she felt her body swell with a wanting as intense as their first time. "Were you looking for me?" she murmured against the lips now on hers.

"Not a bit."

She felt his smile. "Not even a little?" she asked on a sigh.

"Nope." Brady turned her and gathered her in his arms. "Aching for you."

While Brady headed for a luncheon interview with the city's newest hockey player, Maggie took Conor with her to her grandfather's house. An expedition with him meant lugging a diaper bag filled with necessities and a tote bag with toys. She also loaded his riding car into her trunk.

Standing in the driveway while Maggie fastened Conor in the car seat, Renie hooted a laugh. "You look like all the other mothers in the neighborhood chauffeuring their kids. Most of the time, they pack enough in the car for ballet lessons and soccer games to be gone a week."

It was an image Maggie had never anticipated for herself. It was one she reveled in now. She wasn't Conor's mommy, but she felt like it. She couldn't have loved the little boy more if he were her own. "He needs a lot to keep him busy," she finally responded as she slid behind the steering wheel.

"I could have looked after him while you went about your business."

"No. I want him with me," Maggie said honestly.

Renie's eyes smiled at her. "If I haven't told you yet, I like you, Maggie."

Maggie reached out and touched her arm affectionately. "I like you, too."

"Go on now," Renie said, a little gruffer. "You've got things to do."

Maggie had always had plenty to keep her busy. She taught at the university, volunteered for charities, held secretarial and treasurer positions on several committees, chaired benefits, but she'd never felt such contentment, such brightness in her life before, and she knew it was because of Brady and Conor and a life-style that felt comfortable and satisfying.

She was bound by the love she felt for both of them. *Love.* It had crept up on her when she wasn't looking. Brady had changed her life; he'd changed her. Because of him, she wanted everything she'd denied for herself—love, a real marriage, family.

Amazing, she mused as she pulled up to the curb in front of her grandfather's house. All the certainty she'd had that she would never feel love for anyone had been in vain. She'd become as foolish as her mother. No, that wasn't true. Unlike her, Maggie would never make promises.

Carrying Conor into the house, she was pleased to see the workmen were on schedule. The roof was done, and the clanging of a wrench in the bathroom announced that the plumber was busily at work. She'd sunk a good amount of money in the house. A house she might lose. The possibility existed that Cassandra's lawyer might still determine a way to prove that love hadn't inspired her marriage to Brady.

With the sound of the carpenter's hammer banging away, Maggie ushered Conor out to the backyard. While she pulled weeds from the flower garden, he wheeled his yellow-and-orange car around the terrace. She'd never intended to live in this house. Elegant in style, it deserved to be admired by others. It pained her to think of a bulldozer ripping it apart or digging up the flowers she'd tended so unfailingly.

The arrangement with Brady would succeed. She would keep the house and get it listed with the National Historical Register. Conor would live in the warm and happy atmosphere of his father's home. But no happily-ever-after ending. She wouldn't believe in one. That didn't mean, she realized as Conor joined her and knelt beside her, that her heart wouldn't ache when this was over.

* * *

Brady finished the lunch interview. He'd had a hard time concentrating. The court hearing in days plagued his mind with fear. What if the court didn't believe in his and Maggie's marriage? He'd counted on it viewing them as the logical ones, a loving two-parent household, to raise Conor permanently.

Even if the court chose them, what would happen when he and Maggie split? He swore softly under his breath. The thought of that made him want to beg her to love him, not just for Conor's sake but for them.

He'd thought she'd been happy with him. Sometimes his heart pounded as if it might burst through his chest while they were making love. She made him tremble, ache. She made him want to crush her to him with a need that went beyond the passion filling him. He wanted to shout how much he loved her, and was afraid of the risk, afraid he would blink and she would be gone.

Cursing himself, Brady sidestepped several people coming in the restaurant doors. How could he give up all he'd found with her? How could he convince her that he and Conor were incomplete without her? Pausing at the door, he waited until two elderly couples passed him. His intentions to move forward and outside ended with the sight of Olivia.

Her lips pursed, she stalled in the doorway and blocked Brady's escape. "I cannot believe how much damage you have done in such a short time."

Conversations with her often left him baffled, but this one confused him more than usual. "What are you talking about?"

"My grandson. I saw what you have done to him."

"What do you mean, you saw?" Brady asked tiredly.

"When I came to your home, I—"

"When?" he asked, puzzled. "When were you there?"

"The other day. Are you so obtuse that you didn't notice I took Kirsten's duck candy dish?" she said sharply.

Brady didn't give a damn about the antique. He'd kept it for one sentimental reason. Kirsten had loved it. "What did you want?"

"To see my grandson." Her back visibly stiffened. "Clearly you have already ruined him. He's become quite unmanageable."

Several people glanced their way, making her aware she'd raised her voice.

Brady spoke quietly. What was going on between them was private. "There's *nothing* wrong with him."

Her chin lifted a notch. "Of course you wouldn't think so."

Brady had had enough. He would be damned if he would let her spoil his day. "He's mine, and I'll raise him the way I want, and that means with a lot of love," he said, before turning his back on her and stepping outside.

He took several deep breaths, then dashed to his car. All he wanted to do was get home and be with his wife and son. Seeing Olivia had reminded him that time might be the enemy for them now.

Maggie returned home before dinner. With Conor playing on the living room floor and zooming his truck underneath chair legs, she'd planned to read. She barely got the book open when the phone rang. "I've got it, Renie," she yelled out before offering the caller a greeting.

"Darling, it's Mother," the caller said cheerfully. "That is you, isn't it, Margaret?"

Maggie sank back into a chair at the sound of her mother's voice.

"I'm getting married again," she said in that girlish, breezy voice she had when excited.

When had she divorced the last one? Maggie tried to remember.

"Just like my little girl," she gushed.

Maggie had never been her little girl.

"Are you happy, Margaret? I hope so. I want everyone to be as happy as I am."

Maggie was slow to answer. She couldn't ever remember her mother asking her that question. "Yes, I am."

"I'm glad. Love does that to a woman. I love being in love, though I'm not very good at it," she said with an amused laugh at herself. Humor still etched her voice. "I was a terrible disappointment to your father. All of the Buchanans were so stable, so—" She laughed in an airy way. "So boring. You're so like them. Oh, dear," she quickly amended. "I didn't mean—"

"It's all right. I understand," Maggie said, certain she would never really understand her mother.

"Thank you. I suppose you do. You were always so mature, even as a little girl. I had no idea how to talk to you."

Because you never tried, Mother.

"Andrew is a retired Realtor from Florida living in Spain now," she rambled, describing her latest love. "We have a villa, and we'll probably get married next month some time."

Is that why she'd called, to tell her about the wedding?

Maggie wondered. "I didn't thank you for the wedding gift you sent Brady and me."

"Oh, well, actually, that's why I called. I'm—this is terribly embarrassing, Margaret, but I'm short of funds, as they say. At least, until I get married. If you haven't deposited the—"

Maggie cut in, guessing what her mother was working up the courage to say. "I won't cash the check."

"Thank you. It will only be for a month, then I'll send you another."

"You don't have to." *I need nothing from you.* "I'm well taken care of."

There was a second of silence. "Of course you are. The Buchanan money is all yours now, isn't it?"

Maggie felt a tightness in her chest as she waited for her mother to express a word of sympathy about Maggie's grandfather.

She said nothing. Instead, she uncharacteristically stammered. "Per—perhaps—" Again, silence.

"You need money?"

"Just a little to hold me over. Till next month," she said lightly.

"Until you're married?"

"Yes, precisely."

Maggie made the expected offer. "Would five thousand be enough?"

"That would help a great deal."

Suddenly weary, Maggie engineered the conversation toward a quick ending. "I'll send a check."

"Margaret?"

"Yes." Now what? Maggie wondered.

"I meant it when I said that I never knew how to talk to you," she said, sounding more serious. "You were so like your father. But now—" The smile returned to her voice. "Now that you're a woman, it's easier. I would like to call again."

Maggie gripped the receiver tighter. Why? Why did those words mean so much to her? "When you get a chance."

"After the honeymoon," her mother said gaily again.

"Yes, all right. You can tell me all about it," Maggie answered. But she wasn't too hopeful her mother would remember. She'd never been great at keeping promises.

With her mother's breezy goodbye, Maggie set down the receiver. She'd lied to herself, she realized. She still loved her mother, but she might never really like her.

Glancing at her watch, she noted it was almost time for Brady to come home. The past wasn't a part of her life anymore. Now she had a husband and son to think about.

She dashed to the bathroom, showered and was settled with Conor playing his favorite game of catching fish when Brady arrived.

Dinner was chaotic, between Conor spilling his milk and the phone ringing twice. Bennett called, once to remind them about tomorrow night's masquerade party, and the next time to ask Brady for his CPA's phone number.

"Let's do something tonight," Brady urged, lounging against the kitchen sink as he set the receiver back in its cradle. "I'll go stir-crazy if I don't."

Was he worrying about their day in court? Maggie wanted to ask. "What do you want to do?"

"We could go to a movie."

She had no problem with the idea, but she doubted his choice would be a movie she would want to see. She also was surprised. Since coming home, he'd spent almost every minute with Conor. She hadn't expected him to want any separation from his son, even to leave him for a few hours in Renie's care while they went to a movie.

"I thought we'd go to a drive-in," he said, folding the newspaper open to the theater section. "Then Conor can go with us."

Maggie smiled. Either he'd become more predictable, or, through closeness with him these past weeks, she'd become more attuned to him. "What movie?" She was prepared to play parent if he chose the wrong one.

"Conor hasn't seen the movie with the dalmatians, and there's a shorter movie with it." He set the newspaper down. "Something or other about chipmunks."

In Maggie's mind, he deserved a Best Daddy prize. "Won't you be bored?"

"I like dogs." He squatted beside his son and ruffled his hair. "And Conor will like it."

"Sounds fine to me." But Maggie knew Conor's attention span. Forty-five minutes to an hour, tops.

"If we go to the late show..." Brady paused and

snagged up a few toys. "He'll probably fall asleep while watching it," he went on as he dropped the toys into Conor's toy box.

"Then *we'll* be watching two chipmunks chasing each other," Maggie said on a laugh as she gathered up the rest of the toys strewn around the living room.

"I had other ideas." Brady brought his hand to her face and tilted his head to nuzzle her neck. An ache slithered through him for her.

"Such as?" she teased.

His mouth hovered above hers. Taunting himself, he brushed his lips across hers and satisfied himself with only a sampling of her sweetness. "I thought we'd neck."

"You have great ideas," Maggie murmured.

In her whole life, Maggie had never been to a drive-in theater. That wasn't something she would admit to anyone. She didn't consider herself a snob, but her girlfriends in school tended to prefer the ballet and symphony, and she would never have gone to one with a boyfriend. Drive-ins meant fending off a boy's advances.

After moving Conor's car seat in front so he could see the movie better, Brady took off to buy popcorn. Maggie laughed when he returned with two giant-size cups, plus a treat for Conor.

"Candy?" Conor asked as his father settled behind the steering wheel.

"I got him the kind where the chocolate won't get messy on his hands," he told a watchful Maggie.

She stifled a smile at his serious paternal expression

and shrugged. "You're the one who'll pay the dentist bills."

"Ah, Maggie." He handed her one of the popcorn containers. "You can't be sensible about what you eat at the movies."

I'm always sensible, she could have told him. Even her mother said so.

"You're quiet," he said softly, looking at her over the top of Conor's head as he sat between them. "Because your mother called?"

Maggie swung a look at him. "How...? Never mind. Renie told you," she said knowingly.

"She said she hadn't been eavesdropping. She heard you say 'Mother' when you were on the phone."

"It's okay," Maggie assured him. "I know she cares about us." And since Renie hadn't told Brady what she'd known about Kirsten, she'd probably felt that if there were no secrets, her marriage to Brady would keep on the right track. Of course, Renie didn't know the real reason for the marriage.

"You don't want to talk about it?" She meant too much to him for him to let this pass.

"There's not much to tell." Hurt. She would never not feel it when she talked about her mother, but at least it didn't consume her anymore.

"How can you say that? She called after seven years. She must have wanted to talk to you."

"The phone call wasn't really about her and me. It was about her and a lack of money." Maggie saw no point in mentioning that her mother had also asked for a handout. "She took back her wedding gift to us."

Brady mentally shook his head. The look on her face tugged at his heart. How could someone so insensitive produce such a thoughtful and kind woman as Maggie?

In the dark car, Maggie touched his hand on the steering wheel. "I think I've finally learned to accept who she is." Quiet, she stared at the screen. Nothing would ever change her relationship with her mother. And she felt sorry for her, always looking for happiness and never finding it. To end the concern she read in his eyes, she steered the conversation away from herself. "Did your interview go well?"

Brady followed her lead that she didn't want to say more about the phone call. "It was a good one. But I ran into someone when I was leaving the restaurant."

Maggie heard the edge in his voice and made a guess. "Olivia?"

"Never a pleasant experience." He peered at her. "She said she came to the house yesterday."

Maggie winced. She'd meant to tell him, but after he'd overheard Renie's words about Kirsten, Maggie had been more concerned with his feelings than Olivia's visit. "I'm sorry, I forgot to mention it."

"Dog," Conor yelled, pointing toward the screen. "More."

Maggie laughed. "Lots more," she said as a dozen of the black-spotted pups raced across the screen.

"Lots," Conor repeated.

Brady kept staring at her, waiting until her attention came back to him. "She said something about Conor being unmanageable."

Maggie silently cursed the woman. "She doesn't

possess enough maternal instincts to fit in a thimble. She expects a two-year-old to act as if he's six.''

This wasn't news to Brady. Olivia's unrealistic expectations of Conor scared the hell out of Brady.

''When he wouldn't come to her, she got angry.''

''Did she frighten him?''

Maggie stalled. ''For a minute, Brady, but that soon passed,'' she said quickly, to keep him calm since the incident was over with.

''Damn her,'' Brady muttered.

Conor's head jerked his way.

''Dang. Dang. Dang her,'' Brady said, as if trying to convince his son that's originally what he'd said.

Maggie stifled a laugh. ''You got away with that this time,'' she said, noting that Conor was engrossed in the movie again. ''But don't expect to as he gets older.''

''More dogs,'' Conor shouted.

Maggie turned her attention to the movie. How right this night seemed, like so many others, just because she was with them.

Within half an hour, the soft sound of Conor snoring filled the car.

Brady opened the car door and leaned in to move Conor and the car seat. ''I'll put him in the back, so we can get more comfortable.''

More comfortable sounded good to her. While Brady refastened Conor's car seat in back, Maggie scooted closer to the steering wheel.

''We could skip that masquerade thing tomorrow night,'' Brady said when he slid in beside her. He wanted to be alone with his son and her, not passing inconsequential conversation with others.

Maggie squinched her nose. ''Oh, my gosh, I forgot about the costumes.''

Brady draped an arm on the seat behind her. ''So did I—deliberately.''

Maggie ignored his grumbling tone. ''I hate to think what we're going to have to wear.''

''We could skip it,'' he said hopefully.

She thought he needed a reminder. ''Bennett said we need to go.''

''Let's forget Bennett for now.'' As she angled her face toward his, he lowered his mouth to hers. Slowly, tenderly, he kissed her.

''Is this necking time?''

Brady curbed the longing within him to tell her they belonged together, could have a great life together. But he could give her desire; she would accept that from him. ''Long overdue today,'' he murmured, before bringing his mouth down harder on hers.

Chapter Twelve

Brady yawned for the third time since he'd arrived at the newspaper, and stretched around his computer keyboard for his coffee. He drained the last of the cold brew in the foam cup, then hit the save button on his keyboard and leaned back in his chair. The column contained tidbits about trades, manager changes, player discontent and a strike threat. Once a week, he devoted the column to news around the leagues. Though it usually proved the easiest column to write, gathering the information for it required flitting in and out of different restaurants frequented by team members, or catching a player between airplane flights, or conveniently running into another at some night spot.

Since his marriage to Maggie, he'd curtailed his nightlife and had done much of the information gathering while on road trips with the city's sports teams.

Tomorrow was his day off. No column would appear in the following day's newspaper. Brady balled a sheet of notes and tossed it into his wastebasket. Just as well. He would be busy enough on Monday in the courthouse. What if he and Maggie entered it, and by some fluke, Olivia had proof that they'd never intended for their marriage to last forever? Under his breath, he swore. For now, he needed to stop looking for trouble or he would drive himself crazy.

"You've got a visitor, McQueen," Charlie said.

Brady jerked his thoughts back to his surroundings. "Who's that bear?"

"Bear?" Certain the usually gruff-speaking man at the desk beside him was losing his grip on reality, Brady swung a look around.

"Right there." His cigar anchored between his teeth, Charlie grinned and motioned at Conor dressed as Winnie the Pooh.

His little hand holding Maggie's, he yelled from desks away, "Da."

Brady shoved back his chair to meet his son halfway.

He dashed to him, the orange, pumpkin-shaped bag dangling from his hand banging against his little leg. "Twiks or twet," he yelled out.

Maggie waited while Brady scooped him into his arms and Conor delivered his greeting hug. "I hope you don't mind that we stopped by."

"And miss seeing him like this?" Around him, Brady heard a few oohs and aahs, and comments about how cute Conor was. "Hardly."

"I don't have any honey," Charlie mumbled around his cigar, referring to Conor dressed like a bear. "But I have a piece of candy in my desk." He gave Conor a closed-lipped grin and looked at Maggie for permission.

"I don't think a piece will hurt. They served ice cream and cake at the party."

"That's right." Brady sent her a knowing smile. "You two went to a party today." The quick roll of Maggie's eyes amused him. "Was Lannie Heatherford in top form?"

"Unbearably. She's determined the world never forgets her family has ties to England's royal family. She had Misty dressed in an ermine cape and a little tiara."

"Makes me eager to see how Lannie is going to come to the masquerade party tonight."

"Last year, Lannie and Grayson Heatherford came as King Arthur and Queen Guinevere."

Lightly Brady tickled Conor to stir his son's giggle. "So who are we going as?"

"I meant to go to the costume shop earlier, but I didn't want Conor to miss the party." Maggie gazed at the clock, then opened her arms for Conor. "We'd better leave or we'll be scrounging around the house for something to wear."

With his cigar, Charlie gestured toward Brady. "You could go as a hobo."

Maggie smiled with Brady. "No, he couldn't. Invitations stated that the costumes have to depict a character from history, books or the movies."

Charlie pushed back his squeaky chair. "Sounds like one of those classy bashes."

"*The* event of the fall season," Maggie stated. "It raises funds for the animal shelters."

In an uncharacteristic and unexpected move, Charlie offered a gentlemanly arm to Maggie. "I'll walk you out, and you can tell me more about it."

Maggie laughed. "That's the nicest suggestion anyone has made to me all day."

Looking pleased, Charlie pointed a finger back at Brady.

"You could be replaced if you're not careful."

"Unlikely," Maggie said, and in the true spirit of a newlywed absolutely crazy about her spouse, she bent forward and gave Brady a quick kiss goodbye.

The warmth of her mouth lingering on his, he stared after her and Conor strolling out with Charlie. Around him, a few co-workers smiled approvingly about the affectionate gesture they'd seen. This was what the whole plan was about, wasn't it? Pretend to be in love, madly in love. Only he didn't have to act anymore.

"Trick or treat," three little voices rang out as Maggie opened the door.

Maggie dropped small candy bars into each bag held out toward her. Thank-yous followed. She watched a ballerina, a Ninja Turtle and a gorilla scurry away from the house to join their watchful parents who stood on the sidewalk.

"I'll take over," Renie volunteered, "or do you want me to get Conor ready for bed?"

Since they'd talked the other day, a closeness had developed between them. "I'll bathe Conor."

"Figured you'd want to," Renie replied, and reached for the candy dish as the doorbell rang.

The nightly ritual with Conor lasted longer than

expected. He dawdled in the bathtub, wiggled while Maggie tried to slip on his pajama top and downright refused the bottoms. With emphasis, he adamantly said the word *no* to everything. Because he had a sweet, cooperative personality, Maggie had wondered if he sensed Brady's and her tension about the upcoming court hearing.

Behind her, the door opened. Maggie kept her attention on a wiggly Conor. The woodsy scent of Brady's aftershave reached her before he sidled close.

"Are you almost ready?" Over her shoulder, Brady watched her deftly fasten Conor's diaper.

"I will be in a few minutes. I had this changed, but he needed it done again."

"I'll put on his pajamas," Brady volunteered.

Maggie stepped back to let him take her place. "He's in a mood," she sang out before wandering into the bedroom to dress for the masquerade ball. Even if she rushed to get into her costume, they'd be fashionably late for the party.

While she checked her image in the mirror, from across the hall she heard Brady reading a bedtime story about a bear family going camping. Dressed in a tan suede dress for her portrayal as Pocahontas, Maggie critically viewed her backside in the mirror. The skirt was short, the fringed hem stopping between her thighs and kneecaps. She brushed her hair straight, added a beaded headband and slipped her feet into soft doe-colored slippers. Except for being chilly tonight because of the costume's brevity, she would be comfortable. She doubted that was true for her Captain John Smith. Making a last adjustment to the headband, she traced her steps to Conor's room. Asleep, he looked so sweet and peaceful.

"I definitely want to forget this," Brady suddenly announced on a whisper. Stopping beside her, he gently ran a hand over his son's head.

Maggie let her gaze sweep over him. He looked dashing in the snug breeches and knee-high boots.

"You keep looking at me like that, and—"

Maggie silenced him with a quick kiss, then bent over to kiss Conor good-night. At the touch of Brady's hand on her hip, she released a soft laugh. "Bennett said that—"

"You're being too serious again," he teased as she laid her head against his shoulder.

Laughingly, Maggie pointed out, "You always say that when you know I'm right."

"No, I don't."

Maggie slipped away from his embrace. "Of course you do." She breezed past him to the door. "We have to go. But—"

"But what?"

A teasing spirit sweeping over her, she shot a look over her shoulder. "We could leave early."

As she predicted, they arrived late. Some familiar faces hid behind masks. Maggie instantly identified the director of the local animal shelter. Costumed as a dalmatian, he was following his rotund wife who was garbed in fake fur as Cruella de Vil. Three different couples dressed as Scarlett and Rhett. In true form, Lannie chose royalty this year for her and her husband, and they glided around the dance floor as Cinderella and Prince Charming.

"The gang's all here," Brady murmured while they stood on the fringe of the party. He eyed one of several buffets set out in opened pine coffins. Besides caviar, they contained miniature hor d'oeuvres that taunted a man's appetite and made him wish for a hamburger. From one of a dozen Draculas serving drinks, he snatched a glass of champagne off a tray.

"I really do love coming to this every year. It's fascinating."

"The costumes?" he asked while ushering Maggie past several couples mirroring each other in Cleopatra and Mark Antony costumes.

"Seeing what different people choose." Maggie watched a man garbed as Napoleon. "We should mingle."

"Let's dance first."

"We've never danced before."

"At the wedding," he said, gathering her close.

In his arms, Maggie curled a hand at the back of his neck and concentrated on following him. She'd never considered herself a great dancer. "We only did a few steps."

As she ran her hand in a caress over the hair at his nape, heat radiated through Brady. People filled the room; he saw only her. She was a part of him now. "Don't worry." Lightly his fingers skimmed her back. "We already know we move well together."

Maggie thought of all the other times he'd held her. "We do, don't we?" she said a little dreamily. Slowly he circled the floor with her. Around them, voices buzzed with conversation, ice cubes clinked in glasses, and the music drifted through the air. A languid, relaxed sensation, as if she were drugged, floated over her. She'd never expected too much. She'd learned that few things were lasting, but for a few moments while in his arms, she wanted to let her emotions run free, she wanted to believe in them.

"Your friend is coming near."

With her attention shifting toward Deidre, Maggie stepped on his toes. "I'm really terrible at this."

"You feel wonderful in my arms." Brady kissed the tip of her nose. Because of her, tension about the court appearance had seeped out of him.

"I hope you still feel that way when your toes are aching later." Maggie held the smile on her face for Deidre and Henry, who were gliding closer to talk. "That is such a wonderful costume," Maggie said to her. Charming, she thought. Deidre was dressed as Eliza Doolittle, the flower girl from *My Fair Lady*. Wearing a green fitted jacket, green skirt and floral apron, she fiddled with the fresh violets in the basket she carried as she and Henry faced them. Wearing a brown herringbone suit with a vest and tweed hat, he looked just as pedantic as Professor Henry Higgins.

"And you both look—" Deidre sighed and giggled. "You look so in love."

Maggie managed another smile before Deidre and Henry danced away. Love. Her parents, too, must have believed they were in love at the beginning of their marriage. "She's one of the people I'll need to apologize to when—when I can tell the truth." No longer did she want to think when this was over. At no response from Brady, she looked up. He appeared deep in thought. Despite his smiling at the right moments, more than once she'd seen a distant expression clouding his eyes, as if his mind had wandered. "Are you nervous about the hearing Monday?"

Scared. "Conor is where he belongs," he said firmly. "The court will realize that." All night, he'd dodged what needed to be said to her. "But the court hearing won't put an end to this. You know we can't separate right away." Brady had come up with lots of good reasons for them to stay together. What he hadn't done was say the words that were in his heart, the words he knew she wouldn't want to hear.

Relaxing against him, Maggie avoided thoughts about the inevitable. For a little while longer, she just wanted to enjoy herself. But that thought was short-lived. In his ear, she hissed like a cornered cat as she watched Cassandra sauntering toward them, her hoop skirt swaying.

Pulling back, Brady spotted her cousin, and with the last notes of the music, he steered Maggie toward the edge of the dance floor.

"You're both doing great," a voice said behind them.

Her eyes on her cousin, Maggie jumped, startled, and whirled around toward her brother. "I like your earring," she teased. In pirate garb, he looked dashing with a patch over his eye.

"Who are you supposed to be?" Brady asked.

"Any pirate, matey," he said in a gruff voice. He winked at Maggie. "You look cute." His eyes shifted to Brady and he swept a look over him.

"Don't you say a word about these pants," Brady warned his friend.

"Not me. I'm poured into these, too." The laughter eased out of Bennett's voice as he grabbed Brady's arm. "One of the hockey players is here with his wife. Introduce me. Maggie can handle our sweet cousin better by herself."

Brady balked at leaving her alone.

"It might be best," Maggie said, aware her cousin would be scrutinizing their every look or action.

Reassuringly, Brady squeezed her hand. "I'll be back as soon as your brother's through getting autographs."

Maggie laughed with him, but it took effort to keep a smile plastered on her face for her cousin's benefit.

"Quaint costume," Cassandra said snidely. "You're aware that everyone is talking about you."

"Are they?"

She presented a tight-lipped, pleased smile. "This won't work. The house will be mine, Margaret."

She sounded so convinced, almost as if she knew something that Maggie didn't. In the past Maggie had ignored her clipped tone. Now it annoyed her.

"Everyone knows that this was an arranged marriage." Looking down, she adjusted the narrow silk cuff on her dress. "Certainly you have nothing in common." She swept a look over the guests and visually zeroed in on Brady. "I'm sorry if this sounds cruel, Margaret, but you simply don't have what if takes to hold a man like that."

"Since we are married, you're obviously wrong."

Her cousin's mouth noticeably tightened. "Oh, puleeze. Don't play the act for me. Eventually, I'll have the proof that this is a sham."

Maggie raised her chin a notch. "I'm his wife in every way."

"Oh, my dear, how naive you are. Brady has a reputation for—

"That was before."

Cassandra's eyes widened slightly. "Why, I'm beginning to believe that you really think this marriage is for real. Did he fool you into believing he loved you? Margaret, he only wants you because of the custody battle for his son. When he loses to Olivia," she said with amused sarcasm, "your husband won't even need you anymore. He'll leave you. He'll have made a laughingstock out of you."

Across the room, Brady started to inch himself away from Bennett and another man, an avid Phoenix Suns fan who droned on about the team's need for a tall center as if he knew more than all the coaches. His politeness stretched to its limit, Brady excused himself, then quickly weaved his way around people to reach Maggie. "Hi," he said softly.

Still digesting what Cassandra had said, Maggie took a second before meeting Brady's gaze. "Hi, yourself."

"Did you need me?"

He had no idea how much. Maggie gave him a slim smile. "My cousin was at her best."

Possessively, he ran a hand down her back and guided her toward the dancers. "Want to tell me what happened with her?"

Maggie moved with him onto the crowded dance floor. "Cassandra believes she'll get proof, that everyone will know she's right about our marriage. I'm wondering what she's going to do to try to discredit the marriage."

"She won't win," he said, as much for himself as

her. "Believe me. Because regardless of what happens with Conor, I won't let you down."

She wouldn't hold him to that promise. But she was touched by it. She doubted either of her parents had ever spoken those words.

"We've seen everyone," Brady murmured near her ear. "And everyone has seen us."

Maggie swayed back against his arm to angle a look up at him and gave him a bright smile. "Think we could leave now?"

Brady bent his head and planted a kiss on her brow. "I thought you'd never suggest it."

Morning sunshine warmed the bedroom. After a dreary gray Sunday, Maggie hoped this morning's brightness was an omen of more sunny days ahead. Caught in tangled sheets, Maggie squinted and nuzzled closer to Brady. "It's almost time for Conor to start announcing he's awake," she said sleepily.

"Uh-huh." He spoke in a husky morning voice.

It was a sound she sensed she would long for when this was over. Tilting her head, she saw a pleasurable expression on his face. And with no thought but of now, Maggie wrapped around him and closed her eyes. Beneath her, she felt the steadiness of his breaths. Emotions dominated her. She doubted now that memories would be enough, and for a little while longer, just a little while, she wanted to believe in them.

Even when Maggie later eased from his embrace, Brady resisted opening his eyes. With her no longer beside him, a lousy mood slipped over him. Hearing the sound of the shower, he buried his head beneath the pillow. By evening, he would be in the pits of depression or flying high with happiness at having permanent custody of his son again. But what about Maggie and him?

"Da, Da, Da," Conor chanted from across the hall.

On a low groan, Brady rubbed a hand over his unshaven chin, then tossed off the sheet. "Coming," he yelled to his son while he dragged on his jeans. Not bothering with shoes, he padded barefoot to Conor's bedroom.

"Da." Conor greeted him with his usual grin. "Up."

"You're taking after Maggie. Both of you need to learn the fine art of sleeping later."

"Ater," his son repeated.

Brady grinned at the arms stretched out to him. "Are you hungry?"

"Eat. Peza."

"No. No pizza." He nuzzled Conor's neck and lifted him from the bed. "Let's get that diaper changed."

Patient while Brady dressed him, Conor sat still until Brady was tying his second shoe. "Go."

Laughing at his impatience, Brady hoisted him high above his head. "We're going." With Conor on his shoulders, he dashed toward the kitchen. To him, the greatest sound in the world was his son's belly laugh. But would this be the last morning he'd have an opportunity to greet his son, to do something silly with him?

He had to stop thinking that way. Conor wasn't going anywhere. Tonight he would tuck him into his bed in the bedroom with its baseball wallpaper. Tonight and every night after, he would stop to check on his son before going to bed himself.

Thoughts drifted back to Maggie. Would that bed be empty? He knew it didn't have to be, and found the mess he was in ironic. So many women had been a part of his life before Kirsten. He'd settled down with her, been faithful to her, but since her death, he'd enjoyed his bachelor status. Ironically, they'd all wanted one thing from him, the one thing Maggie shunned—love.

A heck of a mess. He settled Conor in his high chair, then poured whipped eggs into a frying pan. He was in love with a woman who planned to split from his life in months. The calendar hanging on the wall near the refrigerator mocked him. Below a photograph of a famous running back barreling for the end zone, bold letters announced November. Less than thirty days from today, they would celebrate Maggie's birthday. She would also gain ownership of the house she loved so much. Bargain finished. She would leave soon after.

"Milk," Conor called from his high chair.

"Coming up." Brady flung open the refrigerator door to retrieve the milk. "We got problems, Conor," he said while pouring the milk into a plastic glass. "Maggie needs us, and she doesn't know it."

"Aggie?"

Brady set the glass before his son. "Yeah, Maggie." He couldn't deny how special she was. Everything would be easier if she were ordinary, if what they'd shared had amounted to nothing. But he and Conor needed her, not for any dumb agreement, or for the sake of appearances. He needed to see her face first thing in the morning, hear her laughter. He needed more moments of watching her brush her hair or enjoying the sight of her wriggling into a pair of jeans. He needed more memories of the sound of her humming some silly song to Conor. He needed her, because without her, his heart was empty.

Nerves. Maggie couldn't quell them while she dressed. At the ring of the telephone behind her, she actually jumped. Frowning at herself, she whirled away from the mirror and snatched up the receiver.

Sounding brighter than she felt, her brother returned her greeting. "I was checking to make sure you two were up. You can't afford to be late."

"We won't be. Have I ever been late in my life?"

He chuckled in response. "No, you haven't, but Brady's not Mr. Punctuality."

"We'll be on time."

He offered a few encouraging words that she supposed all lawyers learned to utter to clients before court appearances. One of his words of wisdom included not acting nervous. Maggie wondered if that was possible. One little boy's future hinged on Brady and her presenting the perfect image of Mommy and Daddy.

Again, her stomach tensed. Relax. Try to relax, she berated herself, and smoothed down her suit jacket. Wandering out of the bedroom, she followed a trail of Conor's toys and picked them up on her way to the kitchen.

Seated in his high chair, he looked like such a big boy, holding a plastic cup with a lid and a straw. He wouldn't be a baby much longer. Soon he would be riding his first bike. She wished—she wished with all her heart that she would be around to see the many firsts in his life. "You got up earlier than usual."

"And conveniently while you were in the shower." Brady ended his search in a kitchen drawer for Conor's spoon and turned to see her kissing Conor's chubby cheek. "Stinky morning diaper." She flashed a smile at him that never reached her eyes. What was she thinking about today? Like him, was she masking anxiety? Was she scared, too? He couldn't fathom coming home without Conor in his arms.

"Bennett called." Maggie accepted the coffee cup that he handed her. "Thank you. He said that he would meet us at the courthouse." She took a sip, then set the cup down to hold her arms out away from her sides. "Do I look all right?"

"Terrific." With some amusement, he watched the hint of a blush brighten her cheeks.

"No. You know what I meant. Is this outfit okay?" She'd deliberately chosen a sedate hunter green suit and a cream-colored, round-necked blouse. Olivia always dressed in conservative navy blue or gray outfits. And always wore a single strand of pearls.

"Traditional." She looked so proper with her hair caught up and secured at the back of her head that he wanted to mess her up a little. "Irresistible."

"Thank you, but that's not the image I want," Maggie countered.

"Irresistible to me," he said softly. "And I'm not just saying that because—" He paused, aware of how close he'd come to blurting out his feelings. Saying I love you meant breaking a rule of their agreement. Keep everything normal, don't panic her, he warned himself. He slid eggs onto plates for both of them. He tended to push too much, too quickly. He couldn't afford to do that with her. He had time yet to convince her that what they'd found by accident some people searched all their lives for.

Maggie checked the clock. Time ticked by so slowly when turmoil existed. "Did Bennett say anything to you about who he would bring to court to vouch for us?"

"He might not need anyone. But Renie will be there." Brady placed her plate on the table. "That's why I'm cooking. She's getting dressed."

Maggie felt that Renie was an unknown factor. "Do you think she believes us?"

Brady shrugged in an attempt to mask his own anxiety. "Why wouldn't she?" He and Maggie had talked and laughed and slept together. Often enough, he had had a difficult time remembering this wasn't for keeps.

"Bennett mentioned that he might call Charlie." Maggie poured cereal into a bowl for Conor. "I like him."

Brady straddled a chair across from her. "He's an old-fashioned newsman." He continued the inconsequential conversation to keep their minds free of tenser thoughts. "The gruff steamroller type."

Maggie spread her napkin across her lap. "He's fond of you."

"Think so?" He worked at a smile as he joined her at the table.

"I know so."

"He must have done a good sell job on himself with you."

She held her fork in midair. ''Actually, he talked about you.''

Questioningly, Brady regarded her over the rim of his coffee cup. ''Did he?''

''Yes.'' Maggie deliberately teased him, poking her fork into her eggs and taking her time to answer. Like him, she was trying hard for normalcy. ''He said you're a very nice man,'' she said more seriously. ''I knew that, but he told me things you've done for other people.''

Brady shrugged. ''He tends to exaggerate.''

With someone else, she might have viewed such a response as that of someone with false modesty. She knew him better. He usually reacted honestly. While what he'd done was admirable, she assumed that he truly didn't think of his actions as anything above the normal. Maggie believed differently. ''He said you have a soft heart. But I knew that, too.''

Brady sent her a wry grin. ''He's usually not such a blabbermouth.''

She said no more, sensing he would shrug away any importance in what he'd done. But there was something special about a man who raced around the city to get tickets to a big football game for a waitress at the diner around the corner from the newspaper, a single mother who'd wanted to give her ten-year-old son a memorable birthday present. And there was something deeply caring about a man who found a job for a stranger whom he'd seen sleeping behind a building near the ballpark. And there was also something wonderfully generous about a man who would give up his hotel room to a family stranded because of a snowstorm, even though he had to sleep in the lobby.

"Aren't the eggs any good?" Brady asked, because she'd stopped eating.

"You're not doing much better." With her fork, Maggie gestured at the untouched food on his plate. "I suppose we've both got butterflies in our stomachs."

"All done." Conor nudged away his cereal bowl.

Maggie retrieved a washcloth to wipe off his hands while Brady removed Conor's cereal bowl from the high chair.

As she turned back, so did he. "Maggie." His intense blue eyes pinned her. "Whatever happens in there today—"

"Only one thing is going to happen," Maggie insisted. "Conor is coming home with us."

With us. He wondered if she realized what she'd said. He didn't dare speak about his doubts, for fear they might become real.

While Brady went to shower and dress for their court hearing, Maggie cleaned up the breakfast dishes. She nearly dropped one with Conor's wail. On a run, she reached the living room to see Conor with his hand stuck under the small space beneath the television console. Maggie dropped to her knees and wriggled his hand out.

More scared than hurt, he wailed.

"Sh, it's all right," she soothed, gathering him in her arms.

"Ma-ma, ow."

Maggie's heart stopped. She'd already surmised the injury was nothing serious. But what he'd said was.

"Oh, Conor." At the shopping mall, he'd heard a little girl his age call for her mommy. Maggie hadn't thought the word had registered with him, had meant anything to him. But he wasn't mistaking her for Kirsten. He'd never known his mother. She'd died before he'd started to talk. That wonderful word had been meant for her, for someone who, in his young mind, was the person to hug when something hurt.

"Conor, sweet baby." Maggie shut her eyes as he clung to her as if she were his lifeline. All that she'd denied believing in for most of her life proved false. Deep, consuming love blossomed within her with such intensity she wondered how so much feeling was possible. Tears smarting her eyes, she inhaled the sweetness of him. If the marriage was real, if love existed between her and Brady, she could be a real mother to Conor.

"Maggie, what happened?" In a swift move, Brady crouched beside Conor.

"He hurt his hand," she answered. And she would hurt badly when this was over, she knew now. With her eyes wide open, she'd fallen in love with Brady, and had to expect the heartache when she left. But it hadn't been wise to get so attached to Conor. She should have been more careful. And in that instant, she knew what she had to do. "Brady, I can't stay."

Stroking a thumb across the top of Conor's fingers, Brady swung a look at her. "What are you talking about?"

Because she interpreted what flashed in his eyes as worry, she offered a reassurance. "I wouldn't leave right away. I wouldn't do that to you because of the custody problem."

Something painful rustled within him. It took effort to keep from panicking. "Maggie, I don't know what you're talking about. The agreement we made was meant to last for at least six months."

She understood his concern. If he won today and she left too soon, Olivia could question the motives behind their marriage, and she might convince the court to reverse its ruling. But risk existed for Conor, too, if she stayed.

Brady searched her eyes to try to understand. Did she think she was responsible for Conor getting hurt? "Hey, don't blame yourself for—"

"He didn't hurt himself badly," Maggie cut in. "He was more scared than hurt." Smoothing down Conor's shirt, she avoided looking at Brady. "This isn't about that. I can't stay another month. I have to go." She would have regrets later, but she couldn't stop herself now.

As she disappeared into the kitchen, Brady held Conor until his sniffing stopped, then followed her. Muscles in his back tightened as if preparing for a hard blow. "You can't go." He yearned to say other words. Everything was different now. In such a short time, she'd become too important for him to let her go.

"Brady, I've gone through custody battles."

"That'll be behind us today," he said, trying to make sense when he wanted to beg.

"I know what it's like to ache for your parents, to wait for them to be there. I know what it's like to watch them walk away." .

He shunned emotions churning within him to concentrate harder on the point she was trying to make. "I'm not following you, Maggie."

"Conor is getting confused, Brady," she explained. "He called me Mama."

"He called you Mama?" Is that what this was about? Was she upset that his son had developed such affection for her?

She kept her distance, leaning back against the refrigerator. "If I stay, he'll be hurt."

Anxious, Brady gathered their coffee cups from the table and slid them into the sink. Because of her, he'd found love again. In time, he could make her love him. He just needed more time. "What about your house?"

Maggie didn't care about it anymore. For years, it had been the only place she'd known real happiness. She'd been clinging to it, trying to keep it a part of her life, certain that without it she would lose even those wonderful memories. But she'd found happiness again in another house.

Since she'd married Brady, all that had really mattered to her was seeing that Brady kept Conor. All she had wanted to do was protect Conor, and protect Brady from the agony of losing his son again.

"You'll lose the house, Maggie." Why? Why would she risk everything now? If she left, Cassandra would win.

Maggie said what was in her heart. "A child is more important than a house. If I stay, if Conor gets more attached to me, he'll be hurt when I eventually walk away from him."

She didn't have to. If only he could get her to understand that.

"I don't want to see the same thing happen to Conor that happened to me. If I stay too long, even for the term of the agreement, it could, couldn't it?"

Brady closed the space between them and took her hand. She was doing this for his son. She was going to lose everything she wanted to protect Conor.

"You see I'm right." Before he could answer, Maggie freed her hand from his grip and turned away.

How could he argue to stop her? What could he say when she was right? His son's attachment to her grew stronger each day that she was with them. If they carried out this bargain for the sake of the trust, if she never loved him the way he loved her, Conor might suffer when she left.

Chapter Thirteen

Maggie settled on a chair in family court between her brother and Brady and held Conor on her lap. "We came early because—"

Brady touched her hand to silence her. "Why do you look so worried?" he asked, regarding Bennett's frown.

Maggie, too, noted the deeply etched frown line between her brother's brows.

"We pulled a tough judge," he said quietly.

Determined to stay optimistic, Brady reminded him, "We're a nice traditional family."

"But *you* haven't always been." Bennett looked pained at having to bring up his past.

"That was long ago. Before Conor, before Kirsten." Mentally, he grimaced. That wasn't true. He'd been playing the field with the same gusto since her death as he'd shown prior to their marriage. "I've changed," he added quickly.

"Since marrying me, he has changed. He's a good husband," Maggie said, feeling compelled to come to Brady's defense.

Both men looked her way.

Maggie curled her fingers over his. "Well, you are."

Brady gave her a semblance of a smile, but his attention shifted to Olivia's lawyer sitting at the table across the aisle. Alone, he shuffled papers. Oddly, Olivia wasn't with him yet.

"We have to hope your marriage does the job at giving you a more stable image."

"If you add a but, I'm going to slug you," Brady declared. He couldn't lose Conor.

"No, but—" Bennett smiled. "Sorry. But we do have to hope this particular judge believes it. I wanted you to know that Olivia's lawyer called me last week and told me what information about you that he was going to present to the court."

Brady hunched forward to see around Maggie and scowled at her brother. "Why didn't you say anything about this sooner?"

"What was the point in worrying you ahead of time?"

Brady sighed. "So lay it on me now. What information?"

"He has a list of women you saw during a two-month period. How did you ever do that?" Bennett asked in a tone of first incredulity, then admiration.

Maggie mentally groaned. "That's the past. Why should it matter?"

"Depends on how the judge interprets such actions, and your previous bachelor-on-the-loose reputation. Hopefully he'll see you as a family man now."

"Or a man bound to stray." Brady felt his gut tighten with tension. "What else?"

"Look," Bennett said, "her lawyer will try to portray you as a man who wasn't too responsible, who lived on the edge."

Maggie voiced her thought. "And we have nothing like that on Olivia to present to the court."

"She's pristine," Bennett answered her. "Her lineage dates back to the American Revolution. Her family history is squeaky clean."

Except for Kirsten, Maggie mused. Painful as the subject was and as much as she hated to mention Kirsten's death, she asked, "What about the way Kirsten died?"

Bennett shook his head.

"Olivia had so much to do with her daughter's unhappiness," Maggie said. After learning the truth, she'd told her brother.

Bennett's eyes darted to Brady then returned to her. "I wouldn't want to mention that."

"I know it's awful to drag through the court, but—" Maggie stopped as her brother continued to shake his head.

"What your brother isn't saying," Brady said, "is that the court could believe, since she was married to me at the time, that *I* was the reason she was so miserable."

"But that's not true."

He squeezed her hand, touched that she believed so strongly in him.

Maggie agonized for him. On paper, Olivia, with her wealth and position in the community, appeared to be the one to offer the more secure home life to Conor.

"There's no point in second-guessing." Bennett looked away, distracted as he was beckoned along with Olivia's lawyer to enter the judge's chamber.

"Now what?" Brady questioned.

Her brother shrugged.

Seconds later, he returned to tell them they could go to the cafeteria while he found out what was happening. With half an hour to pass, they left the courtroom. Nerves on edge, they ordered coffee but didn't drink it. Renie arrived then, and to keep Conor from getting too impatient, the three of them walked him up and down hallways. Conversation was useless. They were too worried to pretend differently.

With five minutes to spare, they headed back toward the courtroom. The heels of Maggie's shoes clicked in unison with Brady's quick steps. Outside the courtroom doors, Renie waited.

"Did Bennett definitely decide to use your statement?" Brady asked her now.

"Guess so. That's what he said yesterday," Renie replied with a worried glance at Conor.

And what would the woman say? Maggie wondered. True, she'd become her friend, and Maggie believed she loved Brady like a son, but she couldn't lie. If she'd noticed tension in their marriage, she would have to tell the truth. Maggie's anxiety mounted as the courtroom doors opened and Bennett came out.

"Ben," Conor yelled enthusiastically when he spotted Bennett.

"Hey, Conor." Bennett opened his arms to him and took him from Brady.

"Listen," Renie said without any prompting. "If anyone asks me, I'll tell you what I'm going to say. I never saw two people more in love."

Maggie was aware of Brady's quick look at her. Had her feelings for him been so obvious?

"And they both love the boy," Renie went on. "I'm the housekeeper, but it's also my job to see to Conor's needs. Not long ago, when Brady was out of town for his job, Conor cried in the middle of the night. Maggie was in Conor's room before me. And she stayed with him, holding him until he went back to sleep. I know just by the way she acts that she loves the boy as if he were her own."

Bennett laughed and held up a hand to her. "I believe you."

Restless, Maggie glanced at the clock on a wall. "Shouldn't you be inside?" she asked her brother.

"I was."

Maggie sent him a quizzical look.

"Olivia's decided not to fight for custody."

"What!" Rocked by his words, Brady wondered if he'd misunderstood him.

"Bennett, are you serious?" Maggie asked with disbelief.

"I'm serious." His grin widened. "No custody battle. Olivia decided not to continue."

"I don't believe it." Maggie laughed and flung her arms around Brady's neck. "That's wonderful." She kissed him soundly, but as overjoyed as she was, he appeared puzzled. "Brady, it's over. This is all over."

"I know." Baffled about Olivia's actions, he frowned at Bennett. "Why did Olivia change her mind?"

"I don't know. All her lawyer said was that Olivia had withdrawn her claim."

Brady knew he should be jumping for joy, but he needed to understand why Olivia had changed her mind. Scanning the people in the hallway, he searched for Olivia's lawyer. "I'm going to find out." He touched Maggie's arm. "I'll be right back."

Maggie took Conor from her brother and held him to her. Safe. He was safe from the unhappiness, the regimentation, the harsh expectations that Kirsten had unsuccessfully weathered as a child. Maggie didn't doubt that Olivia had meant well with her rigid, disciplined style of child-raising, but she'd choked joy from her daughter's life. Even the love Brady had felt for Kirsten hadn't been strong enough to rectify the damage, to keep her from self-destructing. Thrilled, Maggie kissed Conor's cheek, then nuzzled his neck until he giggled.

"Maggie, anyone seeing you with him would think he was your son."

Smiling at Conor's delighted sound, she looked up at Bennett and saw Brady walking toward them. A solemnness she'd never seen before was etched in his face. "What did he say?"

Brady was still reeling from the lawyer's words. "Olivia decided Conor was getting older and beginning to show his true personality."

Questioningly, Maggie inclined her head. "What does that mean?"

"I guess what happened the last time she visited him changed her mind."

Maggie hadn't forgotten how badly Conor had behaved. "He'd reacted to her." She shrugged. "He nearly threw a temper tantrum," she admitted.

"He never does that," Brady said.

"No, I know he doesn't."

"He's mischievous, he gets into a lot, but all kids his age do that."

"He burst into tears," Maggie explained. "To be honest, it was as if just being with her made him act like a different child," she said while Brady took Conor from her.

"Let's get out of here," Brady urged, feeling the need for fresh air.

"It doesn't explain why she would simply give up," Maggie said when he opened the door for her and they all stepped outside.

"Now what the lawyer said makes sense." Bennett grinned. "Olivia said that Conor was rowdy and loud and disobedient. She believed he'd taken after his father instead of Kirsten."

Maggie noted that Brady appeared rather proud suddenly.

"So it seemed obvious to her," Brady added with a trace of amusement, "that Conor would never be a proper gentleman." He grinned and kissed his son's cheek, then draped an arm around Maggie's shoulder.

"Da. Car."

"Yeah, we're going to the car."

Bennett slapped his friend on the back. "It all

worked out a lot better than we ever expected." Stopping with them beside their car, he kissed his sister's cheek. "The next hurdle should be a breeze," he said encouragingly, in regards to the trust and the house. "I'll call you tomorrow."

Maggie knew differently but remained silent.

"Thanks, Ben," Brady said before her brother took off in the direction of his car. After weeks of worrying, he couldn't believe it was over. He laughed and hugged his son hard while he tightened his hold on Maggie. "Aren't we lucky?"

Maggie nodded. Conor had acted typically for a boy his age who felt anxiety while with someone he viewed as a stranger.

Brady drew her closer. "He decided his own future." But what was their future? He opened the car door and secured Conor in his car seat. Straightening beside the car, he handed Maggie the car keys. "Will you take Conor home?" He glanced at Bennett who was several rows over, unlocking his car door. "I meant to ask Bennett if he still needed tickets for Friday's basketball game."

"How will you get home?"

"Bennett can drop me off."

Maggie didn't question him further. Since leaving the courthouse, Cassandra's previous words had haunted her. Her cousin had been right. Brady had Conor now; he didn't need her anymore. It was time to get away. Now. Now, while she could still save a piece of her heart.

Brady needed help, fast. He caught up with Bennett before he flicked on the ignition.

Puzzlement slipped over his friend's face as he rolled down the car window. "Something wrong?"

"Plenty." Bent forward, Brady rested a forearm on the window frame. "Your sister told me this morning that she isn't planning to stay with me."

"That was the original idea."

"No, you're not understanding. She wants to leave soon."

"Soon?" Bennett stared blankly at his dashboard. Brady could almost hear the wheels turning in his head. "Did you do something to her?"

Brady glared at him. "I didn't do anything that she didn't want done."

"Then why did she say that?"

"To protect Conor. She's putting Conor's best interests first." Brady met his friend's stare. "Conor called her Mama."

"No kidding?" Bennett grinned. "Well, I'm not surprised that they've gotten close."

Neither was Brady. Only Maggie seemed upset about it.

"I don't see the problem."

"She thinks he could be hurt like she was." Brady shook his head. "It's nuts. She's great with Conor."

"I knew she would be." Bennett shifted and draped an arm over his steering wheel. "She always liked kids."

"She loves him. She might not realize that, but she does. And that's why she thinks she has to leave."

Bennett frowned. "It makes sense that she'd feel that way. If Conor is starting to think of her as his mommy, then he could be hurt. And she wouldn't want him to suffer the way that she did when she was younger."

Brady understood her reasoning. What he needed was help to change her mind.

"She was miserable," Bennett went on. "After losing the custody battle, our mother just split one day. No phone calls, no visits. A card on the holidays. And during the years of the custody fights, it wasn't much better for Maggie. I was older. I'd already started to have a life of my own, but her life was hell. She would depend on being with one of them, only to be shipped off to the other. Six weeks here, six weeks there. I think our father really wanted her, but he was involved in work when she came to visit him, so he was always too busy."

Bennett squinted against the sunlight. "I feel sorry for our mother. She's a woman who'll look for someone to love all her life, and she'll never find that person because she doesn't understand that part of loving is giving."

"Maggie is just the opposite. This is all about her thinking about my son's feelings." Brady felt edgy again. "Ben, what I need from you is help. Tell me how to convince her to stay."

Her brother inclined his head questioningly. "Why would you care now? She met the terms of your agreement and stayed until you got Conor."

"But she's not going to get what she wants."

"Sure she will."

"You're not listening," Brady insisted. "I got the impression she'll leave before her birthday. She won't get the house."

"That would be dumb."

"She isn't thinking about the deal anymore."
Brady waited until his friend met his stare. "Neither
am I. What started as a business deal is different now.
I don't want her to leave." He couldn't imagine not
having her around.

"Wait a minute." Brady had his friend's full attention now. "What are you saying?"

"I've changed my mind."

"Changed your mind?" Bennett narrowed his eyes
as if trying to see inside Brady. "That's not what you
mean. You've changed, haven't you." A sly smile
curved his lips. "That's great. I'd hoped you two
would realize you were perfect for each other."

"You planned this?"

"Sure. Why else would I have suggested it? This
is really great."

"Quit saying that and help me figure out what to
say to her."

Looking more serious Bennett shook his head.
"She'll lose what she wanted."

"I know."

"Why would she, unless—"

"Unless what?"

Bennett smiled again. "Unless she is in love with
you, too."

Before Maggie reached home, Conor was asleep in
the car seat. Love hurt. She loved both of them. She
cared as much about them as herself. Oh, how had
she let this happen? Hadn't she learned that marriage
never lasted, at least not in her family? She couldn't
be like them and make promises, only to break them

later. She knew how fragile love was, how little staying power it had, yet she hadn't been able to resist it.

She put Conor down for a nap, then, alone in the bedroom, she blinked hard against the tears smarting her eyes while she opened dresser drawers. Neatness didn't matter, nothing did. She tossed clothes from the dresser into a suitcase. For tonight, she would take only what she needed. The important thing was that she leave now.

She knew what their agreement had been, but that had been before she'd fallen in love with Brady. Love made a difference. Bending over, she picked up Conor's teddy bear. Foolishly, she'd believed that she could keep love and passion separated. How silly of her to believe that, but she'd heard of other people who'd offered one without the other. Willingly, welcomingly, when she wasn't looking, she'd let Brady and Conor into her life. Closing her eyes, she tightened her embrace on the stuffed bear. Her heart twisting, she breathed hard. How foolish she'd been to believe she could also shut them out of her heart.

Bennett's words had knocked the wind out of Brady. What if she was in love with him?

"Need a ride home?" Bennett asked, pulling Brady from that thought.

Brady nodded and settled on the passenger seat.

"Why don't you tell her that you love her?"

His friend's question ended Brady's distracted viewing of passing scenery. Why didn't he? It was a big chance for him and Conor. Bennett had said he'd changed. He had, but not in the way Bennett had meant. There was a time when he wouldn't have let anything stop him from getting what he wanted, when he'd taken plenty of chances. So why hadn't he taken a chance and told her what she meant to him? Damn coward. He'd convinced himself that she wouldn't want to hear that he loved her. The truth was he'd been afraid to say those words. Maybe it was time to take another big chance now, one worth taking for him and Conor.

"Brady?"

"I hear you."

He had Bennett make one stop before dropping him off at home. With an envelope in his pocket, he opened the front door. Instead of the celebratory dinner Brady had hoped for, he stepped in and saw her suitcases sitting near the front door. The click of her heels made him look up. Her head bent, she was carrying her jacket. Would she have left before he got home? "You're leaving?"

Maggie tensed instantly at the disbelief dulling his eyes. "There's no reason not to." She dropped the jacket onto a chair. "There's no danger that Olivia will file again for custody when she learns we're not together anymore. She doesn't want Conor." She had trouble even saying the words. How could anyone not want the wonderful little boy?

"And you're doing this for Conor?"

"Yes." She averted her eyes, afraid her own might reveal what she wasn't saying to him. She was doing this as much for herself as his son. "I told you that I planned to."

"But I thought you meant—later." Frustration slipped into his voice. "Tomorrow, the day after, next week."

"I need to go now." Since she'd left the courthouse, one sensible thought had worked its way through all the emotion that had been controlling her for days. If she left now, she would make it easier on everyone. She wasn't meant for this life. She might believe in love, but she knew marriage, a forever marriage, meant making promises. Her family didn't know how to keep promises of the heart.

Brady thought of yelling at her, shaking her. If he had woken up sooner, told her he loved her, would this be happening now? The desperation creeping over him intensified. "You can't go, Maggie." He struggled for patience to keep from blurting out too much of what he felt too quickly. "It's dumb not to stay. The house is yours if you stay another month." He caught the slight turn of her shoulder. "Listen, to me. I have something to say. I don't want you to go. I want you to stay for keeps."

Maggie swung around and faced him.

He read confusion on her face. There was no room for anything now but honest feelings. "Maggie, I thought I couldn't love again. No, that's not true. I'd been fooling myself, believing I was full of guilt about Kirsten. But I was hiding beneath the blame." No holding back. Brady knew everything he hoped to have with her was on the line. "That way I didn't have to take any chance, risk loving again." He hesitated, then brushed his knuckles across her soft cheek even as he yearned to gather her into his arms. "I took the coward's way and convinced myself that I wasn't worthy of such love. I'd been feeding myself a bunch of bull because I lacked the guts to love again."

Maggie saw tension and sadness in the grim set of his features. He'd forsaken pride to say that to her. She wanted to raise a hand, to caress his cheek, hold him.

"The big pretense of blame had been my way of never getting hurt again. No love, no loss. For too long, I wouldn't admit to myself that I was afraid to lose again," he said with disgust. "Then I woke up. I was going to lose you, anyway, if I didn't take a risk and tell you what I felt. I came home with one thing to say. I love you," he said softly, wondering how three words could possibly explain how much he needed her with him every minute of his life.

Pressure in her chest made her labor for a breath. "I don't want that from you."

Even as her rejection stung, he ignored his own pain. "You want it as much as I do," he insisted, refusing to believe that she'd felt no emotion during all those nights in his arms when she'd made him tremble with her lovemaking.

"Don't do this," she practically pleaded. How would she resist if he kept insisting? She stepped back to put distance between them. "This was a business agreement. Nothing more."

"Bull." Anger edged his voice. "It stopped being a marriage bargain the first time I kissed you. We both knew then that this wasn't something we could walk away from."

Maggie searched for something to say that made sense, that would make him understand. Love wasn't enough. For a long moment, they stood facing each other, the silence lingering, clinging to the air.

"Maggie." He whispered her name and reached

out to bring her near, to feel her softness, her warmth, but stopped himself. "Maggie, this wasn't something I expected, either." He wished he could touch and ease away the frown marring her brow. "But I couldn't let it go now, not now. Since you've come into my life, I've found something wonderful." He caught her hand and felt relief that she didn't pull away. "It started as a make-believe marriage, but it's real now. Why should we let it go?" he asked appealingly, and gently tugged her closer. "Why?"

One second she was almost in his arms, the next she jerked back as the doorbell rung on the air.

Exasperation snowballed within him. So close. He was so close to holding her. Beneath his breath, he swore and whipped around to answer the door. He would start over as soon as he got rid of whoever was at the door. But she wasn't leaving until he had his say. No, dammit, she wasn't leaving ever.

Flinging open the door, he swore again. The last person either of them needed to see at this moment was Cassandra and her lawyer. "What do you want now?" he asked, greeting her with a frown.

"To see my cousin." She breezed past him.

An apologetic look on his face, her lawyer waited for Brady to step to the side before he followed her in.

"If you'll tell her I'm here, I'll—" She stilled abruptly, unaware of Maggie only feet away as her eyes fixed on the suitcases. "See there." Quickly she recovered from her discovery, glee brightening her eyes. "I told you," she said with a triumphant look, poking a finger in the direction of the luggage. "This is a bogus marriage."

Maggie didn't care. As much as she loved her grandfather's home, she no longer centered her whole life on its restoration. She'd grown since the days when she wanted so desperately to keep possession of it. It was a building, nothing more. She understood now that memories of love, those she'd had with her grandparents, and now with Brady and Conor, were hers forever. No one would ever take them from her.

Cassandra's eyes turned on Maggie. Her chin lifted to an angle that was insulting as she glided closer. "He got what he wanted and dumped you, just like I said, didn't he?" she asked in a low voice, for only Maggie to hear.

Maggie thought of all the years she'd endured Cassandra while growing up when they were at family gatherings. While adults had mingled and conversed, she'd usually sat in a corner and been the recipient of her snobbish cousin's taunts. Withdrawn, shy, she'd never retaliated. Anger suddenly stormed her. "What is happening here is none of your business."

Cassandra drew back as if she'd been punched. Quickly she recovered, her brittle laugh filling the air. "Why, Maggie, I do believe you've grown claws." Looking jubilant, she sauntered back to her lawyer. "We should have no problem. This is no marriage." Her long-nailed hand swept toward the suitcase. "She's leaving him."

Brady caught the flare of annoyance in Maggie's eyes. Enough. Every protective instinct he possessed rose for her. "I don't know why you would think that. With my son's custody no longer an issue, Maggie and I decided to take our postponed honeymoon."

Cassandra cast him a doubtful look. "Honey-moon?"

Incredulity colored Maggie's voice. "Honey-moon?"

"My surprise, darling," he said, stepping close to Maggie and slipping an arm around her waist. Un-buttoning his suit jacket, he fished in his inside pocket and set the envelope in her hand. "Airplane tickets. I stopped on the way home and picked them up. I thought we could both use a change. Does sunny Ha-waii sound all right to you?"

Maggie knew she should play her part, but she was too stunned. Her mind refused to think about anything except why he had bought the tickets.

With her silence, Cassandra, no dummy, jumped in. "The honeymoon is obviously unexpected to you, Maggie. So why *is* your suitcase already packed?"

Brady had had enough of her arrogant tone. "You must lead a boring life, Cassie."

She cringed at the nickname he gave her.

"Doesn't your husband ever do anything sponta-neous?" he mocked. "I told Maggie to go home and pack because I had a surprise for her. I just didn't tell her what that surprise was."

Cassandra's eyes narrowed suspiciously. "I don't believe you."

Brady sent her lawyer a sympathetic look. "She must be a joy to have for a client." Keeping his arm firm on Maggie's waist, he grinned. "Now, if you'll go, I can start packing so we can leave for our va-cation."

"I don't believe it, I don't believe it," Cassandra

muttered, turning toward the door at her lawyer's urging hand beneath her elbow.

"We'll invite you to see the house after we finish restoring it."

She glared back at him, then in a huff, whipped away.

Maggie heard the door shut behind them, but she kept staring at the airplane tickets in her hand. "Why did you do this?" she asked, feeling as stunned now as she had when he handed them to her.

"Because I want to go on one. Because we never had one. Because we need to."

Maggie made a small sound as his arms slipped around her and he drew her against him. She wanted to believe him. Even the thought of one day without him and without Conor made her heart twist. But how could she believe in them? "I'm not meant for this life." She made herself ease from his embrace.

Brady held firm. They belonged together. He was certain that having her with him was more important than anything else.

Maggie's heart quickened. "Brady, I don't want to fail like my parents did. I don't want to hurt a child the way they did."

Gently, he pressed a fingertip to her lips to silence her. "You've already proven you won't," he said softly. "They were selfish people who thought only of themselves. You were willing to give up something important to you for Conor."

"I love him," Maggie admitted, because she could never lie about her feelings for that little boy.

"I know. And he loves you."

Did she dare trust him, trust herself that they could make it last?

"Tell me you don't love me, and I'll let you go."

How could she deny what she felt? "I can't."

"Maggie, believe me," he whispered. "I love you. I love the way you look at me first thing in the morning, the way you touch my son with love, the way you listen intently when I'm rambling about a team's inadequacies. I love you because you're giving, and caring, and you're the most loving woman that I've ever known. So loving, you'd give up everything important to you for us."

Her eyes filling with tears of joy, Maggie shook her head. "You're wrong. All that is important to me—all that matters is you and Conor."

"Say it," he begged, needing to hear the words from her.

"I love you. I love you so much."

He framed her face with his hands and closed his mouth over hers. The kiss was filled with the love she never allowed herself to believe in. As the kiss deepened, she knew, too, that here, with this man and his son, she had found what she thought was impossible. Her mouth clinging to his, she answered his kiss with the love in her heart. There were no guarantees of forever, but in his kiss came a message, a pledge. They'd try. They would never stop trying to make each other happy. She couldn't have asked for more, she knew in that instant.

"I gather that means there's only one thing left to do," he murmured against her lips.

She tilted back her head to meet his eyes squarely. "What's that?"

"I'd better pack a suitcase, too."

Maggie caressed the line of his jaw with her fingertips. "I have one request."

"Anything you want," he said while gently brushing her hair back from her face.

"Get one more ticket for Conor."

"Maggie, you fill my heart. I think I might burst with what I feel for you." As she smiled, so did he. "I'd hoped you'd say that," he said on a soft laugh, and leaned away to reach into his pocket.

Maggie fingered the third airplane ticket. She noted a fourth for Renie still in his pocket. One little boy had opened Brady's and her hearts to love. "Without him, there would have been no us," she murmured before his mouth captured hers again. Joy mingled in with her love. What he'd given her was something precious—a promise, a promise of forever.

* * * * *

THE BABY OF THE MONTH CLUB

RITA Award Winning Author

MARIE FERRARELLA's

*miniseries continues with her
brand-new Silhouette single title*

In The Family Way

Dr. Rafe Saldana was Bedford's most popular pediatrician.
And though the handsome doctor had a whole lot of love for
his tiny patients, his heart wasn't open for business with
women. At least, not until single mother Dana Morrow
walked into his life. But Dana was about to become the
newest member of the Baby of the Month Club. Was the
dashing doctor ready to play daddy to her baby-to-be?

Available June 1998.

Silhouette®

Find this new title by Marie Ferrarella
at your favorite retail outlet.

Look us up on-line at: http://www.romance.net   PSMFIFWAY

#1171 UNEXPECTED MOMMY—Sherryl Woods
That Special Woman!
And Baby Makes Three: The Next Generation
Single father Chance Adams was hell-bent on claiming his share of
the family ranch. Even if it meant trying to seduce his uncle's lovely
stepdaughter. But when Chance fell in love with the spirited beauty for real,
could he convince Jenny to be his wife—and his son's new mommy?

#1172 A FATHER'S VOW—Myrna Temte
Montana Mavericks: Return to Whitehorn
Traditional Native American Sam Brightwater was perfectly content
with his life. Until vivacious schoolteacher Julia Stedman stormed into
Whitehorn and wrapped herself around his hardened heart. With fatherhood
beckoning, Sam vowed to swallow his pride and fight for his woman and
child....

#1173 STALLION TAMER—Lindsay McKenna
Cowboys of the Southwest
Vulnerable Jessica Donovan sought solace on the home front, but what she
found was a soul mate in lone horse wrangler Dan Black. She identified
with the war veteran's pain, as well as with the secret yearning in his eyes.
Would the healing force of their love grant them a beautiful life together?

#1174 PRACTICALLY MARRIED—Christine Rimmer
Conveniently Yours
Rancher Zach Bravo vowed to never get burned by a woman again. But he
knew that soft-spoken single mom Tess DeMarley would be the perfect
wife. And he was positively *livid* at the notion that Tess's heart belonged to
someone else. Could he turn this practical union into a true love match?

#1175 THE PATERNITY QUESTION—Andrea Edwards
Double Wedding
Sophisticated city-dweller Neal Sheridan was elated when he secretly
swapped places with his country-based twin. Until he accidentally agreed to
father gorgeous Lisa Hughes's child! He had no intention of fulfilling that
promise, but could he really resist Lisa's baby-making seduction?

#1176 BABY IN HIS CRADLE—Diana Whitney
Stork Express
On the run from her manipulative ex, very pregnant Ellie Malone wound up
on the doorstep of Samuel Evans's mountain retreat. When the brooding
recluse delivered her baby and tenderly nursed her back to health, her heart
filled with hope. Would love bring joy and laughter back into their lives?

BEVERLY BARTON

**Continues the
twelve-book series—
36 Hours—in April 1998
with Book Ten**

NINE MONTHS

Paige Summers couldn't have been more shocked when she
learned that the man with whom she had spent one passionate,
stormy night was none other than her arrogant new boss! And
just because he was the father of her unborn baby didn't give
him the right to claim her as his wife. Especially when he
wasn't offering the one thing she wanted: his heart.

For Jared and Paige and *all* the residents of Grand Springs,
Colorado, the storm-induced blackout was just the beginning of
36 Hours that changed *everything!* You won't want to miss a
single book.

Available at your favorite retail outlet.

™

Look us up on-line at: http://www.romance.net   SC36HRS10

Catch more great
◆ HARLEQUIN™ Movies
™
featured on **the movie channel** tmc

Premiering April 11th
Hard to Forget
based on the novel by bestselling
Harlequin Superromance® author
Evelyn A. Crowe

Don't miss next month's movie!
Premiering May 9th
The Awakening
starring Cynthia Geary and David Beecroft
based on the novel by Patricia Coughlin

If you are not currently a subscriber to
The Movie Channel, simply call your
local cable or satellite provider for more
details. Call today, and don't miss out
on the romance!

the movie channel tmc

◆ HARLEQUIN™
™ *Makes any time special.*™

100% pure movies.
100% pure fun.

Harlequin, Joey Device, Makes any time special and Superromance are trademarks of
Harlequin Enterprises Limited. The Movie Channel is a service mark of Showtime Networks, Inc.,
a Viacom Company.

An Alliance Television Production

HMBPA498

Silhouette® Books

is proud to announce the arrival of

A MOTHER'S GIFT

This May, for three women, the perfect Mother's Day gift is mother*hood!* With the help of a lonely child in need of a home and the love of a very special man, these three heroines are about to receive this most precious gift as they surrender their single lives for a future as a family.

Waiting for Mom
by Kathleen Eagle
Nobody's Child
by Emilie Richards
Mother's Day Baby
by Joan Elliott Pickart

Three brand-new, heartwarming stories by three of your favorite authors in one collection—it's the best Mother's Day gift the rest of us could hope for.

Available May 1998 at your favorite retail outlet.

Look us up on-line at: http://www.romance.net   PSMOMGFT